Praise for Ja

"An outsider in America, Jack Kerouac was a true original."　　　　　　　　—Ann Charters

"The wonder of Kerouac's muscular, free-form, imagistic language still astonishes. He remains an essential American mythologizer—one caught up in that backstreet world of bohemian life, before it was transformed by the harsh social Darwinism of capitalism . . . A hundred years after his birth, we still want to live that Kerouacian vision of life as one long cool stretch of highway."　　　　　　　　　　　　　　　—*New Statesman*

"Kerouac is more relevant than ever as we mark 100 years since his birth."　　　　　　　　—*The Guardian*

"Kerouac dreams of America in the authentic rolling rhythms of a Whitman or a Thomas Wolfe, drunk with eagerness for life."　　　　　　　　—John K. Hutchens

"*On the Road* is the most beautifully executed, the clearest and the most important utterance yet made by the generation Kerouac himself named years ago as 'beat,' and whose principal avatar he is . . . A major novel."　　　　　　　　　　　　　　　—*New York Times*

"The way that [*On the Road*] is so enduring—so impervious to shifting cultural winds—seems to indicate something about how successfully it articulates a very American rootlessness . . . A hysterical elegy for threatened male freedom . . . Might be the last great American novel about masculine seduction."   —*New Yorker*

"*On the Road* has the kind of drive that blasts through to a large public . . . What makes the novel really important, what gives it that drive is a genuine new, engaging and exciting prose style . . . What keeps the book going is the power and beauty of the writing."
                                                    —*San Francisco Chronicle*

"*Big Sur* is so devastatingly honest and painful and yet so beautifully written . . . He was sharing his pain and suffering with the reader in the same way Dostoevsky did, with the idea of salvation through suffering."
                                                    —David Amram

"In many ways, particularly in the lyrical immediacy that is his distinctive glory, this is Kerouac's best book . . . Certainly, he has never displayed more 'gentle sweetness.'"   —*San Francisco Chronicle*, on *Big Sur*

"Kerouac's grittiest novel to date and the one which will be read with most respect by those skeptical of all the Beat business in the first place."
                                                    —*New York Times Book Review*, on *Big Sur*

PIC

PIC

JACK KEROUAC

Grove Press
New York

Printed in the United States of America

This Grove Atlantic paperback edition: January 2024

ISBN 978-0-8021-6083-6
eISBN 978-0-8021-6084-3

Library of Congress Cataloging-in-Publication data is available for this
title.

Grove Press
an imprint of Grove Atlantic
154 West 14th Street
New York, NY 10011

Distributed by Publishers Group West

groveatlantic.com

24 25 26 27 28   10 9 8 7 6 5 4 3 2 1

Dedicated to Dr. Danny DeSole

CONTENTS

PIC

1. ME AND GRANDPA

AIN'T NEVER NOBODY LOVED ME like I love myself, cept my mother and she's dead. (My grandpa, he's so old he can remember a hunnerd years back but what happened last week and the day before, he don't know.) My pa gone away so long ago ain't nobody remember what his face like. My brother, ever' Sunday afternoon in his new suit in front of the house, out on that old road, and grandpa and me just set on the porch rockin and talkin, but my brother paid it no mind and one day he was gone and ain't never been back.

Grandpa, when we was alone, said he'd ten' the pigs and I go mend the fence yonder, and said, "I seed the Lawd come thu that fence a hunnerd years ago and He shall come again." My Aunt Gastonia come by buttin and puffin said that it was all right, she believed it too,

1

she'd seen the Lord more times than they could ever count, and hallelujahed and hallelujahed, said "While's all this the Gospel word and true, little Pictorial Review Jackson" (that's me) "must go to school to learn and read and write," and grandpa looked at her plum in the eye like if'n to spit tobacco juice in it, and answered, "Thass awright wif me," jess like that, "but that ain't the Lawd's school he's goin' to and he shall never mend his fences."

So I went to school, and came on home from school the afternoon after it and seed nobody would ever know where I come from, if what they called it was North Carolina. It didn't feel like no North Carolina to me. They said I was the darkest, blackest boy ever come to that school. I always knowed *that*, cause I seen white boys come by my house, and I seed pink boys, and I seed blue boys, and I seed green boys, and I seed orange boys, then black, but never seed one so black as me.

Well, I gave this no never mind, and 'joyed myself and made some purty pies when I was awful little till I seed it rully did smell awful bad; and all that, and grandpa a-grinnin from the porch, and smokin his old green pipe. One day two white boys came by seed me and said I was verily black as nigger chiles go. Well, I said that I knowed *that* indeedy. They said they seed I was too small for what they was about, which I now forget, and I said it was a mighty fine frog peekin from his hand. He said

2

it was no frog, but a TOAD, and said TOAD like to make me jump a hunnerd miles high, he said it so plain and loud, and they skedaddled over the hill back of my grandpa's property. So I knew they was a North Carolina, and they was a *toad*, and I dreamed of it 'at night.

On the crossroads Mr. Dunaston let me and old hound dog sit on the steps of his store ever' blessed evenin and I heard the purty singin on the radio just as *plain*, and just as *good*, and learned me two, th'ee, seben songs and sing them. Here come Mr. Otis one time in his big old au-to, bought me two bottles Dr. Pepper, en I took one home to grandpa: *he* said Mr. Otis was a mighty fine man and he knowed his pappy and his pappy's pappy clear back a hunnerd years, and they was good folks. Well, I knowed *that:* and we 'greed, and 'greed Dr. Pepper allus did make a spankin' good fizzle for folkses' moufs. Y'all can tell how I 'joyed myself then.

Well here's all where it was laid out. My grandpa's house, it was all lean-down and 'bout to break, made of sawed planks sawed when they was new from the woods and here they was all wore out like poor dead stumplewood and heavin out in the middle. The roof was like to slip offen its hinges and fall on my grandpa's head. He make it no mind and set there, rockin. The inside of the house was clean like a ear of old dry corn, and jess as crinkly and dead and good for me barefoot as y'all seed if you tried it. Grandpa and me sleep in the big old tinkle-bed and gots room all over, it's so big. Hound dog sleep in the door. Never did close that door till winter come. I cut the wood, grandpa light it into stove. Set there eatin peas and greens and sassmeat and here's a BIG spoon and eat a lot till my belly's all out — when they was a lot. Well, Aunt Gastonia, she bring us food, here, there, last week, next month. Bring us sassmeat, storebread, streak-a-lean. Grandpa grow the peas in the field, and grow the corn field by the fence, and then we fetched the pigs what we grind outen our moufs cause we no cain't chaw it. Hound dog, eat too. House set in the middle of the field. Yonder's the road, sand road all wore hard and pebbly, and the mules comin by and every now'n then a big au-to thrown up a fine cloud a mile high and me smellin it ever'where and sayin to myself, "Now what fo the Lawd don't make hisself mo clean?" Then I snups out me nose, Shah! Well, over yonder is Mr. Dunaston's store at the crossroads, and then the piney woods wif old crow settin ever' mornin on the branch jess cra-a-cra-a-kin, to beat hisself, and me say cra-cra-cra-cra jess like he do, and I gotsa laugh, ever' morning, hee hee hee, it tickle me so. Then yonder th' other way is Mr. Dunaston's brother's tobacco, n'a big, big house Mr. Otis live in, and Miz Bell's house in the middler the field and Miz Bell she like to be as old as grandpa and smoke the pipe jess like he do. Well, she like me. Ever' night ever'body sleep in this house and that house and ever' house, and the only thing you can hear is a old owl—hooo! hooo!—out in the woods, and yek! yek! yek! all the bats, and the yowlin hound dogs, 'n the cricket-bugs a-creekin' in the dark. Then there's the choo-choo out by TOWN, y'know. Only thing you can't hear is a old spider spinnin his cobweb. I go on in the shanty and break a cobweb—after I wipe myself that old spider, he make 'nother cobweb for me. Up yonder in the sky, they's a hunnerd motion stars and here on the ground hit's as *wet*, as like to'd rain. I gets me in the bed and grandpa say, "Boy, keep your big wet feet from me!" but in a little bitty while my feets is dry and I'se tucked in good. Then I see the stars thu the window n' I sleep good.

Y'all can tell how I 'joyed myself then?

2. WHAT HAPPENED

Po GRANDPA, he never get up one mornin, and ever'body come over from Aunt Gastonia's and said he was 'bout to die of misery. On grandpa's pillow I laid my head down and HE tell me it ain't so. And he yell to the Lord to git ever'body outen the house except the good hound dog. Hound dog set a-whinin' under the bed and lick grandpa in the hand. Aunt Gastonia shoo him out. "Hound dog, shoo!" Aunt Gastonia wash my face at the pump. Aunt Gastonia, she put the rag in my ear and stop up the ear and take her finger and turn and turn till I'se 'bout to die. Well, I cry. Grandpa cry too. Aunt Gastonia's son, he run and he run down that road and pooty soon, here come Aunt Gastonia's son run and run back up the road and zip-zip I never seed nobody run s'fast. Then here come Mr. Otis in his big old au-to and pull up right in

front of the house. Well, he was a pow'ful tall man with
yaller hair, you know, and *he* 'membered me, and says,
"Well there, what's to become of you, li'l boy?"

Then he take grandpa by the hand, and roll up his
eyeballs, and fish in the black satchel fo a thing he listen
with, and listen, and ever'body else lean close and listen, and Aunt Gastonia slap her son away, and Mr. Otis
'bout to tap grandpa with one hand under th' other on
grandpa's chest, when him and grandpa gits they eyes
fixed on theirselves all sow'ful and Mr. Otis stop what
he doing. "Ah, old man," Mr. Otis say to grandpa, "and
how have you been?" And grandpa show his yaller teeth
in a grin and he say, and he cackle, "Yonder's the pipe,
hit's a pow'ful smokin-pipe," and wink at Mr. Otis.
Nobody know what he talk like that fo, but Mr. Otis *he*
know and grandpa he laugh so much he jess shake like
the tree when the possum climb up in it. Mr. Otis says
"Where?" and grandpa point to the shelf, still a-cacklin
and 'joyin Mr. Otis so. Well, he sho liked Mr. Otis ever
so much. Up yonder on the shelf so high I never seed
it, Mr. Otis fetched a pipe they was talkin about. It was
made outen corncob and it was the biggenest best pipe
grandpa made. Mr. Otis, he look at it so sow'ful I never
seed that man so. He say "Five years," and that's all he
say, 'case that was the last time he seed grandpa, and
grandpa knowed it.

After a bit, grandpa fell asleep, and ever'body stand aroun talkin till I cain't see how anybody can sleep, and here's what they said. They said grandpa was mighty sick and would die for sho, and me, li'l Pic, well what was they t'do with me? Oh, it was a tar'ble lot of cryin they was doin Aunt Gastonia and her friend Miz Jones, 'case they loved grandpa like I do, the son *he* cry too, and all the little bitty chiles that come in the door from the road t'see. Hound dog, he whined outdoor t'come in. Mr. Otis, he told ever'body t'stop worryin' their minds so, mebbe grandpa be all right soon, but he'd no fo-sure about it, so he's gwine see about sendin grandpa to the *hospital*, and there he be all right. Ever'body 'gree this is what to do and's grateful to Mr. Otis, 'case he pay with all his money t'see grandpa try to get good again. "The boy," he say, t'Aunt Gastonia, "you sure your husband and your father see eye to eye with you 'bout keepin that boy?" and she say, "The Lord shall bring mercy unto them." And Mr. Otis say, "Well, I don't reckon it will be so but you take good care of him, hear, and let me know if ever'thing's all right." Lordy, I cry when I heard ever'thing and ever'body talkin so. Oh Lordy, I cry when they takes poor grandpa and carry him to the car like some old sick run-over hound dog and lay him in the back seat, and carry him off to the *hospital.* I cry, Aunt Gastonia she close grandpa's door, and *he* never

8

close it, never did once close it for a hunnerd years. The tar'ble fear make me sick and like to drop on the ground and dig me a hole and cry in it, n'hide, 'case I never seen anything but this house and grandpa all my born days, and here they come draggin me away from th' empty house and my grandpa's done died on me and can't help hisself dyin. Oh Lord, and I remember what he say 'bout the fence and the Lord, and 'bout Mr. Otis and 'bout my big wet feet, and remember him so awful recent and him s'far gone, I cry, and shame ever'body.

3. AUNT GASTONIA'S HOUSE

WELL, THEY TAKES ME DOWN THE ROAD to Aunt Gastonia's house, and it's a big old busted house 'case they's eleben, twell folks livin there, from down the littlest baby-chile up to old Grandpa Jelkey 'at sits inside the house all old and blind. It ain't like grandpa's house no way. Is all them windows roundabout and a big brick chimbley, and the porch, it go clean around the house and chairs on it, and watermelon rinds and sand on the boards so's a body can't roll hisself without. My, I never seed such many flies in all my born days like I seed in that house. No, I don't wantsa stay here. Trees in the barnyard, and cherry tree, and the good swing, but they's six, seben chiles all squealin and squawkin and the pigs is not so good as grandpa's pigs never nohow. I never seed nothin so tedious. No, I don't wantsa stay here. Gots no place to sleep at night exceptin in one bed with th'ee, fo boys, and I can't sleep with they elbows in my face.

Grandpa Jelkey, that man scare me 'case he say "Bring that boy here," and they brings me, and he take a holt of me by th' arms and look at me with one great big yaller eye but don't aim it right, poor thing, and look clear over my head and can't see nothing. Th' other eye, it ain't there no more, th' eyeball sunk inside his head. He got no eyes, that old man. He holt me tight and hurt me, and he say, "This here is the boy. Well, I ain't gots to touch the boy more'n one time a day." Aunt Gastonia, she run up and pull me off. "Why you wantsa curse that boy when y'already cursed ever'body seven times? It ain't his fault what his father done to your eyes, he's jess a chile." And Grandpa Jelkey, he shout up "I'se gwine touch him seben times afore he dies, ain't nobody stop me." "You ain't neither," Aunt Gastonia shout up, and Uncle Sim that's Aunt Gastonia's husband he gotsa take Aunt Gastonia outdoor, and me, I gotsa run and hide in the barnyard, 'case I'se sho scared Grandpa Jelkey reach out and catch me again. Nos'r, I don't like Aunt Gastonia's house, no.

Serpentine Grandpa Jelkey sit in the corner and eat offen his knee and ever'body else eat 'round the table-top, and Grandpa Jelkey hear ever'body talkin, and say "Is that you, boy?" and mean me. I hide b'hind Aunt Gastonia. "Come on stand by me, boy, so's I can touch you twicet. T'won't leave me none but four, and then you pays the curse." "Never pay no mind whad he say," Aunt Gastonia say to me. Uncle Sim he don't say nothin, and he never *look* at me neither, and I'se so scared and so sickly, well, I don't expect I'd a-lived in Aunt Gastonia's house long but t'go die in the woods and being so lowly and blue. Aunt Gastonia say I gits sick and lose eleben pounds, I'se so awful and feeble and lain in the dust all day. "What for you wantsa cry in the dirt, chile," say to me, "and git all that mud on your face like that?" She gotsa wipe the mud. Aunt Gastonia, it wasn't ever her, it was Grandpa Jelkey, and Uncle Simeon, and all the chiles th'ow sand at me. And ain't *nobody* take me see grandpa in the hospital. "Oh Lord, I gotsa stop cryin so."

Grandpa Jelkey, he reach out the window and cotch me and hurt me so I'se fall down dead, and he yell, and he whoop, and he say, "Now I'se cotch the boy and now I done touch him twicet!"—Then he say, then he say, "Th'ee!—fo!—" and Aunt Gastonia she yank me away s'hard I fall in the ground. "I done seed the sign, when I reach out to cotch him," Grandpa Jelkey yell, "and ain't but th'ee left now." Aunt Gastonia bust out cryin and fall on the bed and thrash hesself and don't know what and all the chiles run down the road t'git Uncle Sim what's in the field with the mule, and he come runnin

12

to the road. Lordy, then that old Grandpa Jelkey come
out on the porch lookin f'me and spread his arms, f'me,
and he come right straight t'where I is standin like he
was not blind nohow, but then he stumble over the chair
and yowl out, fall down and hurt hisself. Ever'body say
Oh! Uncle Sim pick up th' old man and carry him in the
house and put him on the bed, and th' old man gaspin.
Uncle Simeon, he told cousin take me outdoor, so me
and cousin go stand outdoor, and hear Uncle Sim and
Aunt Gastonia a-yellin at each other.

"What fo you wantsa keep that boy in this house what
has the curse laid on him, fool woman?" Uncle Sim yell.
And Aunt Gastonia, she pray and she pray, "Oh Lord,
he jess a chile, he ain't done a thing t'nobody, what for
the Lord bring shame and destruction on the head of a
innocent lamb, and a leastest chile." "I ain't got nothin
to do with what the Lord decide," yell Uncle Sim. Aunt
Gastonia say "Lord God, his blood is my blood, and my
sister's blood is my blood, Oh Lord, dear Jesus, save us
from sin, save my husband from sin, save my father-'n-
law from sin, save my chillun from sin, and Lord, dear
Lord, save ME, Gastonia Jelkey, from sin." Uncle Sim,
he come out on the porch and give the blackenest look,
and walk away, 'case Aunt Gastonia she pray all night
now, and *he* don't got nothing to say. Grandpa Jelkey,
he fall asleep.

Well cousin older'n me take me down the road and show me TOWN out yonder, 'case he knowed I'se so forlorn. He say, "Tonight Satty night, ever'body git drunk and go to TOWN yonder and they *rocks,* thass what they do, yas'r." I say, "What you mean *rocks?*" He say, "Boy, they gots jumpin-music and jamboree-singin and dancin all that truck. Yas'r, I seed it Satty night, had some barbecue pig and daddy he drink the bottle down like 'is"—and he throw his big head back, cousin, and he have the biggenest head, y'know, and show me, and say—"WHooee!" Then he jump around a-holtin hisself by the arms t'show me, and he say, "This here dancin. B'you cain't go to no jamboree 'case you gotsa curse on you." So me'n cousin go down the road a bit, and they's all the lights of TOWN I ain't never seed before, and we sits up in the apple tree and sees all that. But I is so low-down it don't make no neither much to me. Lordy, what's I care about all that old town?

Well, cousin go thisaway and I go thataway, and I traipse back up the woods and down the hill to Mr. Dunaston's store, and hear me some radio singin again. Then, you bet, I go way down that road t'grandpa's house. It's all so still, s'empty, well, ain't nobody know it but I is 'bout to die and go to my death in the ground. Old hound dog yowlin at grandpa's door, but *he* ain't livin there, and I ain't livin there neither, ain't nobody livin 'bout it, and he yowl his soul.

Well, grandpa seed the Lord come thu the fence a hunnerd years ago, and now he gotsa die in the hospital and never get t'see no fence nor nothin no more. I ask to th' Lord, "What for the Lord do it to po grandpa?"

I cain't remember no more 'bout Aunt Gastonia's house and ever'thing done happened there.

4. BROTHER COME TO FETCH ME

A BOY LIKE ME AIN'T GOT NO PLACE TO SLEEP lessen he stay where he's at, and I sho didn't wantsa stay at Aunt Gastonia's no more, but jess ain't was nowhere for me to sleep but that po woman's house, so I traipse back thu the black woods, yes'r and there she is, Aunt Gastonia, waitin up f'me with the oil lamp in the kitchen. "Sleep, my chile," she say to me, and so kindly I'se like to fall and sleep on her knee, like I done on my mother's knee when I'se a little bitty chile, before she got die. "Aunt Gastonia take care of you no matter what," she say, and stroke m'head, and I fall asleep.

Well, I'se sick in the bed for two, th'ee, seben days and it rain and rain all the time and Aunt Gastonia feed me grits and sugar and heat up collard greens for me. Grandpa Jelkey, he sit on the other side of the house and say "Bring that boy to me," but ain't nobody bring me to him nor tell him where I is, and Aunt Gastonia tell ever'body to shush. Grandpa Jelkey cotch cousin thu the window like he done me, and he say, "Nope, I reckon this ain't the boy." And cousin he howl like I did.

I sleep two days, and don't wake up none but for to sleep again, and Aunt Gastonia she send cousin to fetch Mr. Otis, but Mr. Otis he gone up NORTH. "Where he gone up NORTH?" she say to cousin, and cousin say, "Why he jess gone up NORTH." "What part the NORTH he gone up there?" and cousin say, "Why, he's gone up to NORTH VIRGINIA." Aunt Gastonia, she bow her po head down and don't know whatsa do.

So Mr. Otis is gone, and Aunt Gastonia pray for me, and bring Miz Jones to pray for me too.

Uncle Sim, he look at me once, and he say to Aunt Gastonia, "That boy's 'bout to folly his grandaddy I reckon," and she look up to the roof and say, "Amen, the world ain't fit for no such a lamb, Jesus save his soul." "Well," say Uncle Sim, "I don't guess it's but one less mouf t'feed," and she shriek "Oh Jehovah guide my man from sinful ways." "Shush your mouf, woman, this man ain't got no time for sinful ways and he ain't a-gonna get no new stove this winter neither, 'case that tobacco patch been cursed, hear, the bugs done started eatin leaves since that boy been here." And he stomp out the door.

17

Well, thass the longest talk I ever hear that man make.

I lay in the bed one Satty mornin, and WHOOP! they's ever'body yellin and talkin outdoor, and carryin on so loud I try to see and stretch my head way out but cain't see nothin. They all comes traipsin up the porch. Well I pull my head back 'case I'se sick. Well, who do you guess come in that door, and all the chillun grinnin behind?

If it ain't my brother, dog my cats, and he change so much since he go away from me and grandpa, I cain't for sure say *who* that man is standin in the door, 'case he gots a little bitty round hat on his head with a little bitty button on top of it, and hairs a-hangin from his chin p'culiar, and he all thin, and lean, and all drew-out tall, and sorry-lookin too. He laugh and laugh when he see me, and come over to the bed for t'catch me, and look at me in th'eye. "Here he is," he say, and it ain't nobody he talk it to, 'case he say it to hisself, and smile, and me, I'se so s'prised I don't say nothin. Well, y'know, I'se so s'prised it make me sit up in the bed.

All the chillun is grinnin, but Aunt Gastonia she trouble and fuss hesself, poor soul, and she keep lookin over her shoulder for fear Uncle Sim come up the road, 'case he don't like my brother neither, I don't reckon. "Looky here John, where you been and what's you come here for?" she say to my brother, and he say "Hey now" and jump up and do the most comical shufflin 'bout the house I ever seed, and I laugh, and all the chillun laugh with me, and Grandpa Jelkey, he rare up and say, "What fo ever'body laugh?"

"I come here to fetch Mister Pic, ma'm, and bring him on my *magic carpet* up NORTH to NEW YORK CITY, your grace," he say, and do the most comical bow-down and fetch off his comical hat and show ever'body his head. The chiles and me, we gotsa laugh again and you ain't never seed such 'joyin and laughin. "Who that talkin?" Grandpa Jelkey say, and he say "Why-all's them chillun laugh so?" But ain't nobody tell him.

"How come you here?" Aunt Gastonia ask my brother, and he tuck his hat under his arm and say, "Why, for to get my brother, that's how come," and he don't traipse about no more, and the chillun teeter on th' edge of their feets, 'case they wantsa laugh some more, but now the big folkses solemn actin.

Me, well great day in the mornin, I get up and trample on the bed with m'feet, hear, I cotch m' breath so hard and feel so good. Whoo!

"You dassn't," Aunt Gastonia say to him, and he say "Yes I do, and why do you say I dassn't?" "Why?" Aunt Gastonia say, "and ain't you some no-account man come in here and say you's gwine take this sick chile away from the roof over his head?"

"No roof of his own, Aunt Gastonia," he say, and that woman rare up and yell, "Don't Aunt Gastonia with *me* none, folks around know you's no-account and never did anything b'drink and traipse around the highway ever' blessed night and then jess up and leave when you most was needed by your po old folks. Go away, go away."

"Who that in the house?" Grandpa Jelkey yell, and fuss and pull at th'arms of his chair and look around. Well, you know, me and the chillun don't laugh no more now.

"Lady," say my brother, "how you talk," and Aunt Gastonia she yell, "Don't lady *me,* and don't come here fetchin no chile from outen my roof and learn him the ways of evil like you done learned from your pappy. YES," she yell, "you no better'n your pappy ever was and no better'n no *Jackson* ever was."

Well, I seed all about my life right then. "Who that man in the house?" yell Grandpa Jelkey, and he was so pow'ful mad I ain't never seed that old blind man so mad. He fetch up his cane and holt it tight. Well, right then here come Uncle Sim on the porch, and when that man see my brother standin in the middle of the house his eyes git big they's like chicken eggs, and white, and round, as hard. And he say soft, and p'culiar, "You ain't got no call bein in this house, man, and you knowed that." He don't turn away none but reach behind the door and pull out that old shovel what's leaning there. "Git out of here." Aunt Gastonia cotch her neck quick, and open her mouth to scream, but ain't scarce ready yet, and ever'body wait.

5. SOME ARGUFYIN

WELL, YOU KNOW, my brother he ain't so scared of Mr. Sim with his big old shovel, and say, "I ain't pickin up this here chair to hit nobody with, nor kill nobody 'cause I come here peaceable and quiet, but I'm sure holdin on to this chair so long as you hold that shovel Mr. Jelkey," and he holt up that chair like the man with lion. His eyeballs get red and he don't like so much none of this. Uncle Sim, he look at him, then he look at Aunt Gastonia, and he say, "What's that boy doin here, tell me, hear?"

And she tell him. And he say "Well then, hush up woman," and he turn to my brother and say, "Well go *on*, and go on mighty quick" and he point out the door.

"Get him, Sim," Grandpa Jelkey yell, and he get up from his chair again and holt out his cane, and yell, "Hit him over the head with the stick, boy."

"Sit that old man down," say Uncle Sim but Aunt Gastonia she start wailin and carryin on for me, 'case she don't wants me to leave with my brother, and she say, "No, Sim, no, that boy's sick and go hungry and cotch cold and ever' single thing in the world will happen to him and he'll turn bad, sinful bad, with that man, and the Lord shall drop it on my soul like the hot irons of hell and perdition, on your soul too, and on this house," and she say this rarin up most tearful and pitiful, for me to see, and come over to hold me and hide me from ever'body and kiss me all over. Whoo!

"Put on your clothes Pic," my brother say to me, and Uncle Sim put down the shovel, and my brother put down the chair, and Aunt Gastonia cry and cry, and holt me, poor woman, and I jess can't move an inch I'se so sorry t'see ever'thing come so mean and bad. Well, Uncle Sim, he come over and cotch Aunt Gastonia and pull her 'way from me, and my brother find my shirt and put it on me, and Aunt Gastonia shriek. Lordy, I find my shoes and I find my hole-hat and I'se ready to go, and brother fetch me up piggy-back, and here we go for the door.

Well then, what you supposed happened? Here come Mr. Otis' au-to licketysplit to the door, and out he come and knock on the house, and look in, and say "Well what's this?" and look at ever'body and push his hat back.

Well, here go ever'body talkin at the same time. Aunt Gastonia, she argufy so hard, and explain so loud, and pray so shriekly, ain't nobody else can hear what's goin on, and Mr. Otis listen to her and look at ever'body else most quiet, and don't say nothin. Well, brother put me down 'case he can't scarce stand there with me on his back whilst ever'body yell, and Mr. Otis take my wrist, and listen, then he roll up m'eyeball like he done poor grandpa and look in there, then he back up and look me all over, and say, "Well, 'pears Pic's in good enough health anyway. Now will you explain ever'thing once around again for me?" and, after Aunt Gastonia done that, and he shooked his head yes, uh-huh, yes, uh-huh, he say, "Well, I don't want to interfere with you folks but I don't guess I was wrong when I said it wouldn't ever do to bring the boy here, ma'm, and likewise don't guess he can stay here." He look at Uncle Sim when he say that, and Uncle Sim say, "Yes'r, I don't 'spect, Mr. Otis, ain't been but trouble since he come here." Then Mr. Otis go over and say hello to Grandpa Jelkey, and Grandpa Jelkey say "I'se shore pleased to hear your voice again, Mister Otis" and he jess sit there grinnin from ear to ear 'case Mr. Otis visitin.

Then Mr. Otis say, "I feel I owe it to this child's grandaddy to see he's taken care of proper" and he turn to my brother, and I don't reckon he like my brother no more'n ever'body else, 'case he say, and shake his head, "It don't 'pear to me like you can take care of this child, neither. You got a *job* up north?"

"Yes'r, I got a job," my brother say, and he make a plain face and tuck his hat under his arm again, but Mr. Otis don't 'pear to 'gree with him, and say "Well, is that the only clothes you got to wear when you travel?" and ever'body look at my brother's clothes, which ain't much of a much, and Mr. Otis say, "All you got there is a Army jacket, and there's holes in the side of your pants, and they don't fit right much anyhow because they're all swole up at the legs and come down to your ankles so's I can't see how you can take 'em off, and you've got a red shirt that ain't been washed, and G.I. boots pretty well scraggly by now, and that there *beret* on your head, so how do you ever expect me to believe you've got a job when you come travelin on home like that?"

"Well sir," my brother say, "it's the *style* nowadays in NEW YORK," but that don't satisfy Mr. Otis none, and he say, "Goatee and all? Well, I just got back from New York City myself and I ain't 'shamed to say it was my first time up there, and I don't think it's a fit place for folks to live whether they be white or colored. I don't see any harm takin care of your brother if you stay home, for after all your grandaddy's house IS still standin and you can get a job HOME as well as ever'where else."

"Well sir," my brother say, "I got a wife in New York," and Mr. Otis say quick "Does she work?" and my brother teeter a little bit on that, and say, "Yes, she works," and Mr. Otis say, "Well then who's goin to take care of this child durin the day?" and my brother get red in the eyeball again 'case he can't conjure up no more to say. Well, you know, I has my fingers crossed, 'case I be so pleased when my brother and me was headin for that door, and here I'se stopped dead in that old house again.

"He'll go to *school* in the daytime," my brother say, and give Mr. Otis a look all tuckered-out and s'prised from such some talk, and Mr. Otis, he smile, and he say "Well, I don't cast any doubt on your intentions, but who's goin to watch that child when he comes *home* from school in that NEW YORK *traffic*? Who's goin to help him cross the street in that coldhearted city, see he don't get run over by a truck and such-like? Yes, and where's that boy likely to get some *fresh air* to breathe? And proper friends that don't go about with knives and guns at fourteen? I ain't seen anything like it in all *my* born days. I don't aim to wish such a life on that boy, and don't guess his grand-daddy would neither in these last days of his, and I'm only doin this because I owe it at least to a very old friend of mine who taught me how to fish when I was no higher'n his knee. Well," and he turn to Aunt Gastonia, and heave a sigh all under him,

26

"the only proper thing to do is put him in a good home till he's old enough t' decide for himself." And he pull out a fine book from his coat, and uncork a fine pen, and write most handsome inside it. "First thing in the mornin I'll call up and make whatever arrangements are necessary, and meanwhile the boy can stay here," and he turn to Aunt Gastonia, "because I'm sure, ma'm, you'll see that ever'thing is maintained proper." Yes, and Mr. Otis speak jess as fine and jess as pleasin as that.

But it ain't so pleasin to me none, 'case I don't like to stay in Aunt Gastonia's house 'nother minute, 'nother night, 'nother no time, nor go to no GOOD HOME like Mr. Otis said, nor see m'brother traipse off so lone and blue down the road like he done. Well, he look back over his shoulder, poor brother, ever' now and then, and dust up the sand slow with his ARMY BOOTS, and Aunt Gastonia's chillun they folly him a piece down the road 'case they like him so and wantsa see him shuffle and bow-down some more like he done in the house, but he don't. Mr. Otis stay on the porch talkin to Uncle Sim till my brother gone in the woods, then Mr. Otis get in his big au-to and go.

Well O well, they I was.

6. I GO THU THE WINDOW

COME NIGHTFALL EVER'BODY GO TO BED, and I'se in the bed with my th'ee little bitty cousins and can't sleep none, and say to myself, "Oh me, what happen to me next?" and I'se wearisome for ever'thing and can't neither cry nor nothing no more. Ever'thing I fixed on done run out on me and wasn't nothin I could do. Lord, it was a bad long night.

Well, next thing I know I'se sleepin 'case I wake up and hear the hound dogs yelpin outdoor, and Uncle Sim open the window from where he sleep and sing out "Shet up that snappin and squallin out there," and Aunt Gastonia say, "What for the hound dogs cry?"

And Uncle Sim look, and come back in and say "Y'ere's a black cat spittin in the tree up yonder" and he go back to sleep. Aunt Gastonia she say, "Black cat go

28

'way from my do," and she make the sign, and go back
to sleep likewise.

Then I hear m' little bitty cousin Willis what sleep
by the window say "Who dat?" and I hear, ever so soft,
"Shhh," and I look. Whooee, it's my brother in the window, and me and Willis creep up over little bitty Henry,
and puts our noses to the screen, and then Jonas, he come
too, and put *his* nose to the screen. "It the man done
dance," say little Willis, and he go "Hee hee hee," but
my brother put his finger on his mouth and say "Shhh!"
Here ever'body listen close for Aunt Gastonia and Uncle
Sim, and Grandpa Jelkey y'at sleep in the corner, but
they jess sleepin and snorin, and the hound dogs whine
so they don't hear nothin neither.

"What for you come here Mister Dancin Man?" say
little Willis, and Jonas say "Uh-huh?" and little Henry
wake up and say *Git offen my laig!* awful loud and
ever'body jump back in the bed under the covers and
m' brother duck down behind the window. Well, woof,
you know, I hold up my breath then. But ain't nobody
wake up.

Ever'body rare back up the window, soft.

"Is you gwine shuffle again?" Jonas say, and little bitty
Henry he woke up and seed what was in the window,
and rub his eye, and say, "Ish-yo-gin-shuff-gin?" 'case
he always r'peats what Jonas say. My brother say "Shhh"

29

and little bitty Henry put his finger to his mouth and turn around and nudge *me*, you know, like it was my foot, then ever'body look at my brother again.

"I'se come to get Pic," my brother say thu his hands, "but I come back tomorrow or next year and dance all over fo ever'one of you and give you each fifty cents, hear me now?"

"What fo you don't wantsa dance now?" little Willis say, and Jonas say "Jess a little bit?" and little bitty Henry say "Jiz-il-bit, hmm?" and my brother put his head on one side, and look at ever'body, and say, "Well, I do really b'lieve they's a Heaven somewhere," and he say, "Pic, git in your clothes quiet whilst I dance for these folks," and I do that quick and my brother he shuffle-up soft and dance in the yard in the moonlight and the chiles watch with a great big old s'prised grin on they faces. Well, you never seed such a dance like he done b'neath the moon like that, and no chiles like them seed one neither.

"Shet up that snappin and squallin out there!" yell Uncle Sim from t'other side of the house, and I tell *you*, ever'body duck down again s'fast nobody seed th' other do it. But Uncle Sim, he only mean the hounds, poor sleepin man.

Then ever'body raise up 'nother time again.

Brother undone the screen from the window and say "Shh" and reach in, and Jonas say "Shh" and little Henry say "S" and I cotch brother's neck, and out I go with my head first and then the feet, and dog my cats, and cat my dogs, and looky-here, if I ain't out in that barnyard in the middle of the dark and ready to leave and go.

"Less go," my brother say, and he haul me up on his back like he done in th' afternoon, and we turn around and look at the chiles in the window, and they's so sorry-lookin they's fixin to cry, you know, and my brother know this, and he say, "Don't cry, chillun, 'case me and Pic come back tomorrow or next year and we all have a big fine time t'gether and go down the crick and fish, and eat candy, and th'ow the baseball, and tell tales t' each other, and climb up the tree and *hant* the folks below, and *all* such fine things, you jess wait awhile, you jess see, y'hear me now?"

"Yas'r," Jonas say, and little Henry say, "Yass," and little Willis say "Uh-huh" and off me and m' brother go, 'cross the barnyard and over the fence and into the woods and don't make a sound. Whoo! We gone and done it.

7. WE COME TO TOWN

GRANDPA, IT WAS THE DARKENEST NIGHT 'case the moon got covered over by clouds jess as soon as brother and me reach the woods, and that moon was jess a scant banana moon and showed but scraggy and feeble betwixt the cloudy when it look out. It got cold, too, and I shore was chill. I reckon they was a rainstorm comin to warm me, 'case I don't at all feel so good as I done when we begun. Seem like they was somethin I forgot to do, or somethin I forgot to bring from back at Aunt Gastonia's house, but I knowed they was nothin like that, exceptin I all dreamed it. Lordy why'd I go dass dream such a thing and fret myself there? Way across the woods and thu the black yonder, here come the *train*, but it's pow'ful far off 'case me and brother only getsa hear it when the wind blow, and hear it *wooo*—all long draw-out and goin away, sound like waitin for to get to the hills. Shoo! it was cold, and p'culiar, and black. But my brother, he don't mind.

He carry me thu the woods a space, then he put me down and say, "Woof, boy, I ain't goin to carry you on my back all the way to New York," and we tramp along till we get to the corn field, and then he say, "Here, you sure you can walk all right after bein sick like you was?" and I say "Yas'r, I'se jess a little chill" and walk along.

My brother say, "I get you a coat first thing," and then he say "Get up little boy," and he haul me up on his back again and look around at me out the corner of his eye. "Listen t' me, Pic" he say, "you're every bit sure you want to come along with me ain't you?" and I say "Yas'r."

"Well what for you call me *sir* when you know I'm your brother?"

"Yas'r" I say, and then I cotch myself and say "Yas'r, brother," and don't know what to say. Well, I reckon I was scared for I don't scarce know where we's goin and what happen to me when we get there if we gets there, and it don't sit right to myself to *ask* brother 'at come get me so glad and so pleased like that.

"Listen to me, Pic," he say, "you jess go along with me till we get home and call me *Slim* like ever'body else do, hear?"

"Yas'r, Slim" I say, and then I cotch myself again, and say "Yass, Slim."

"Well there you go" he laugh. "Now say, you seen that black cat back yonder in the Jelkeys' tree that had all them hound dogs barkin at it? I brung it there myself to make them dogs miss me, and didn't it spit, and fetch them up fine and bring us good luck that old black cat? Well, lookout!" Slim say to a tree, and dodge of it, and duck behind it, and bark at it, and go "Fsst!" like a cat, and both of us laugh some. That's the way *he* was, grandpa.

"Po little boy," he say, and give a sigh, and hitch me up higher on his back. "I guess you're as much scared of ever'thing like a grown man is. It's like the man say in the Bible — A fugitive and a vagabond shalt thou be in the earth. You ain't scarce eleven years old and already knowed that, I don't guess you didn't. Well, I come and made a vagabond out of you proper," and we walk along and come to see the lights of town up ahead, and he don't say nothin. Then here we go step on the road.

"Now, I'll tell you where we're goin," my brother say like if he read my mind and see all the troubles in it, and he say, "Then we'll unnerstand each other fine and be friends to go out to the world together. When I heard about grandpa I knowed all the trouble and shame that would come down on your head, Pic, and told Sheila, that's my wife, she'll be your new mother now, and she agreed with me and said—Go down get that poor chile. Well," he said, "Sheila's a mighty fine woman and you see pretty soon. So here I come down South for you 'case I'm the only kin you got left, and you're the only kin I got, baby. Now, you know why Mr. Otis give Grandpa Jackson that shack and that piece of land you was born on?—and why Mr. Otis wanted to help you today?"

"Nos'r, Slim" I say, and I shore wantsa hear it.

"Because your grandpa was born a slave and Mr. Otis' grandpa owned him once, you never knowed that did you?"

"Nos'r, Slim, nobody never told me that," I say, and seem to me I heard folks talk about *slave* one time, and it fetch up recollections, you know.

"Mr. Otis," my brother say, "he's a good man and feels he owes some of the colored folks some help now and then, and he has a nice way by him though it ain't by *me*, and mean well. Ever'body mean well, in their own pitiful way, and Aunt Gastonia mostly, poor woman. Uncle Sim Jelkey ain't no bad man, he's jess poor and can't support no vagabond Pics like you none. He don't too much hate anybody in his inside heart. Old Grandpa Jelkey, he's jess a old crazy man and I don't guess I'd—be crazy too if the same thing happened to me that happened to him. I tell you about that a minute. Well, I don't aim to see you go to no *foster home* like Mr. Otis was fixin to send you today. Now, you know why Aunt Gastonia take you in but the menfolk Jelkeys don't want you?"

Well, I wantsa hear this, and I say "Why that?"

"That's because your daddy, Alpha Jackson, my daddy as well as yours, done blinded old Grandpa Jelkey in a fearsome fight about ten years ago and ain't nothin but bad blood left betwixt the two families. Aunt Gastonia, she was your mother's sister and loved your mother very much all her life, and took care of her right down the end when daddy come out of five years sentence in the work gang, three of 'em in the Dismal Swamp, and never did come back home to her."

"Where'd he go?" I ax my brother, and try to remember my father's face, but it wasn't no use.

"Nobody know," my brother say, and he walk along glum, and he say "Little man, your father was a *wild man* and a *bad man* and that's all he was, or is, and whether he's alive or dead and where-EVER he's at tonight. Your mother's long dead, poor soul, and nobody blamed *her* for becomin crazy and dyin like she done. Boy," my brother say to me, and turn his head to look at me, "you and me come from the *dark*." He said that, and said it jess as glum.

Well, here we come off the sand road and step on the most level and pleasin road I ever seed, and it's got white posts on the side with little bitty jewels shinin where the road go across the creek, and's got a fine white line painted in the middle of it and all such things. Well! And yonder straight ahead's all the lights of town, and here come three, four autos followin each other and havin a fine fast time, zoom, zoom, zoom.

"Well," my brother say, "you still want to come along with me?"

"Yas'r, Slim, I shore do wantsa go with you."

"Boy," he say, "you and me's hittin that old road for the WAY-yonder. Hey, lookout everybody, here we come," and ain't nobody 'round he say that to, but here we go jumpin down the road along two, th'ee white houses, both of us feelin so fine, and my brother say "Here we come to the outskirts of town" and wave his arm and yell "Wheee," and we hoop-de-doop along.

Here we go by a old white house as big as the woods in back of it, and the house got white poles and a porch mighty pleasin to see up front, and ever so many grand windows clear round back, and lights shinin from out the windows on the handsome grassy yard, and my brother say "Yonder's the ancestrial home of General Clay Tucker Jefferson Davis Calhoun retired hero of the Seventeenth Regimental Divisional Brigade of the Confederate Union 'at got hisself shot in the left side tibular tendon and got hisself stickpinned with a Gold Star

Purple Honor of Congress medal and is now a hunnerd years old in his libr'y up yonder writin the Immemoriam Memories of the Gettysburg Shiloh Battle of Smoky Appamatoxburg, whoo!" and he carry on like that with ever'thing, and he don't care.

And here we go jumpin 'longside a regular house, and another regular house, then they's a whole heap of regular houses, and then they get un-regular and all red-rock color and lights pop up ever'where you see. Whoo! I never seed so many lights, and poles, and window-glass, nor so many people walkin on such even and fine roads. "This is town," my brother say, and well, you know, it seem to me jess 'bout then I seed this here TOWN a long time ago with my mother in a au-to, when we come to the movie show one time and I was little and small and couldn't guess to remember such things. And now here I was in town again, but I was growed-up and I was goin out to the *world* with my brother. Well, ever'thing began to be pow'ful fetchin to watch at.

Here we turn thu a black old place and my brother say "This here's the alley you're goin to wait for me in whilst I get some sandwiches for the bus," and he put me down 'case he's all tucker out, and he take my hand and we walk. Here we come to the end of the alley, right across from a road at's all lit-up and brightly, but the alley it's in a shadow for me to wait in. "Yonder's the chicken shack," he say. "I'll go cross the street quick, and don't dass let nobody see you in case the Jelkeys done woke up and fix to send somebody find us, hear? Stand right here," he say, and push me agin the red-rock wall, and set me there, and then off he go toot across that *street*.

Well, grandpa, they I was with my back ain that wall, and look up at the sky betwixt it and th'other wall, and ever'where I turn my ear I hear au-tos, and folkses talkin, and all kind of noises and music, and I tell you, it was the noise of ever'body *doin somethin* at the same time all over with they hands and feet and voices, jess as plain. I never heard it before in the country, exceptin it come to my ear, jess like the water in the crick way yonder in the nighttime, swash, swash, and come most jumble-up and jolly. I'se so still and listenin, seem like *ever'body* doin somethin 'cept me. Across the street is that chicken shack, and it ain't nothin but a little bitty old shack jess like it say, but's got a most pow'ful bright light inside and they's men sittin in front of a long table-top, and they's eatin somethin 'at smell so *good* to me my mouth start waterin right where I is. They's a heap of radio music in there, and I can hear it clear across the street loud, hear the man sing: "*Where you been hiding baby, been looking everywhere, how come you treat me mean, can't you see I care?*" Well, it was fine radio music, the best I ever did hear, and come out of a big box with red and yaller lights turnin round in it. Over the door they was a wheel spin in a screen, and go humm, humm, and behind it a body could hear still another humm-humm from far away and it sound like a biggener wheel than that. Well, I reckon that was the *world wheel* I heard then. Wasn't it, grandpa? Oh, I was jess pleased.

I say to myself, "I jess take two step-ups this *alley*," and I move up along the wall and come to see more of the street. Whoo! It shore was brightly and pleasin.

Then here come my brother out of the chicken shack with a paper bag in his hand, and here come a bunch of men along the street, and they see him and yell, "Hey there Slim, what you doin down from NEW YORK?" And he yell, "Hello there Harry, and hello there Mr. Redtop Tenorman, and hello there Smoky Joe. Well, what you boys up to?" and they say, "Oh, we jess draggin along, you know." And he say, "Ain't heard you boys jump in a *long* time," and they say "Oh, we jump now and then. Say, how you make it with that mustache on your chin?" My brother say, "Oh, jess goin along tryin to have a good time, you know," and they say "Well hey now" and go off down the street and ever'body say see you later.

Yes, I shore liked town and never knowed it was so lively.

Me and brother sneak on down the alley and back to the skirts of town, and skedaddle along feelin good 'case we gets to eat some of them sandwiches soon and 'case brother say we wait for the *bus* by the *junction*, and that bus it's about due any minute, and when we get on that bus I won't be cold no more, and he won't neither. "Bus station ain't no place for us tonight, boy," he says to me, and he say "Oh well, oh well, and who cares, I guess it's all the same when you believe in the Lord like I do, now say, You hear me Lord?"

And we sit on the white posts with the shiny buttons in em and wait 'bout half an hour for the bus, or two half hours, I don't recollect.

Here it come. It come big and brawly in the road, and said "WASHINGTON" on it, and the man at the wheel jam down the speed to stop for us, and it go zoom-boom right by us like it NEVER stop, and spit sand and wind and a old hot smell in my face, but stop yonder jess for us, and we run for it. Well, when I seed that big machine I said to myself "Ain't nobody know where *I'm* goin in this thing but my brother watch over me from now on."

I never see Aunt Gastonia no more now.

8. THE BUS GO UP NORTH

GRANDPA, ain't gonta tell too much about the bus 'case a heap of doins was croppin up in NEW YORK, and I didn't have no notion about em in that bus, and jess gawked, you know.

Well, brother and me paid the man some money, then we walked back thu the people in the seats and ever'body look at us and we look at them, then we sit down in the back sofa, only it ain't rightly a soft sofa, and there we sit lookin straight ahead over ever'body's head at the driver, and he turn off the light and zoom-up the bus, and faster and faster we go with two big old lights leadin us the way thu the land. Brother fall asleep right away, but I stayed awake. I reckon we left *North Carolina* after 'bout a half hour, or two half hours, 'case the road done change from black to brown and on each side of it I didn't get to see

no more houses but jess the wilderness. I guess it was
jess great big old woods without no houses, and dark?
and black? and jess as solemn? It was the *wilderness* Aunt
Gastonia pray about when she pray agin it so loud.

And here come the rain pourin down on that wilderness, and the road run wet and lonesome right thu it.

It was a scarifyin thing to see and make a body glad
he's in a bus with a whole lot of people.

I watched ever'body all night long, but they was most
sleepin in their chairs and it was too black to see, and I
tried to see, but it wasn't no use. I shore didn't wantsa
go to sleep that night.

I say to myself "Pic, you're going to *New York* now,
and ain't it somethin, now ain't it?" and I prod myself,
and feel good.

And I got all sleepy p'culiar in m'eyes 'case I sleep this
time of the evenin back home here, and over to Aunt
Gastonia's too, so next thing I know I jess has to sleep,
and that's all I done that night.

Come 'bout mornin I look up and see where I am,
in the *bus*, and can't believe it, and say to myself "Now
that's why I'se bouncin so dadblame much." And I
look over to brother, and he's still sleepin and's got the
whole back sofa to hisself and's all stretched out loose
and peaceful, and I'se pleased to see him sleep so 'case
I know he must be tired. And I look out the window.

And you know, I never seed anything so pow'ful grand and big, and I seed pow'fuller and grander things since then, all the way to *Californy*. What I seed then was jess like when the first time I seed the *world* I tell you. It was a great river with a tree shore on both sides, and poureds a whole power of water betwixt the land about a mile long, and then it spread out yonder all flat I guess for to pass off to the *sea*. Way yonder on a hill they was a big old white house with posts on the porch like I seed the night before, a *ancestrial* home of a General retired hero of Appamatoxburg like brother said, and on the other side of the river I seed a grand and fearsome housetop, all white and round and jess like a handsome cup upside down, with little bitty far away trees and tiny little roofs rounderneath it. The man in front said to his wife, "Yonder's the Capitol dome darling" and point to it, and that's what it was. And they was the finest, softenest wind blew in from the land to the river, and make ever'thing ripple and jump in the water all over, most peaceful. The sun shine on that grand fine Capitol dome and hit flush on a streamer 'at's tied to a gold pole way on top of it, and do it dazzly, too. All that land I told you we done roll over in the bus all night, here we was in the middle of it, 'case they *never* was a town so white and so laid out grand, and brother woke up and said "This here is the city of *Washington* the nation's capitol where the President of

44

the United States of America and ever'body is," and he rub his eyes, and I look close and can see they's a heap of things goin on yonder in Washington 'case I hear it hum all over when the bus slow down at the river red light and I put my head out the window to watch. Well, and I never seed such a big sky, and so many fine, solemn clouds as passed over Washington of the United States 'at mornin.

After that, grandpa, I didn't get to sleep much. It was mighty hot inside the city of Washington when we stopped there and had to change to another bus 'at said NEW YORK on it, and crowded? Ever'body in the world lined up for that New York bus, and sat inside sweatin. I couldn't sleep no more except on brother's arm, and had to sit up straight in that back sofa and drop my head over most uncomfortable, and his poor shoulder was so hot. Busdriver man say "Baltimore next stop," but run off to do somethin else instead and don't come back f'the longest time. Well, I wished we was back on that NIGHT bus in the WILDERNESS. Babies was cryin all up and down the bus, and felt jess as bad as I did I guess. I look out the window and all I see is the wall on one side, and the wall th'other side, and the sun beat down on the roof, and whew! it was so daggone hot I was sickish. I say to myself "Why don't nobody open a window in here?" and I look around and ever'body's sweatin but don't make a move for the window. I say to Slim "Less open a window or we's dead." And Slim pull and tug and rassle at that window, but can't bulge it one bit. "Phew!" he say. "This must be one of them *modern air-conditioned* buses. Phew!" Slim say "Less go, bus, and blow some air in here." And a man up front turn around and give us a look, then *he* try to open *his* window, and can't bulge it, and sweat and cuss over it. Here come a big soldier-man and he reach out and give that window one big pull-up, and it don't bulge none. So ever'body look straight ahead and go on sweatin.

Well, you know that busdriver man come back and seed Slim pullin some more at that window, and he said "Please leave the windows alone, this happens to be an air-conditioned bus" and he turn on a button up front when he start the bus, and I tell you the finest cool air began to blow all over that bus, only thing is, ever'body got *cold* in a minute and the sweat turns on me like ice water. So Slim, he tugged at that window again to get some *hot air* back in, but couldn't do it, and we look thu the window at them beautiful green fields, and Slim said they was MARYLAND, and wished he was settin in the sunny grass. I reckon ever'body felt the same way too.

Grandpa, travelin ain't the easiest and pleasingest thing in the world but you shore gets to see many innerestin things and don't go 'bout it backwards neither.

When we got to *Philadelphia* folks got out the bus and me and Slim got ourselves a new seat smackdab up front in the driver's window, and bought-up some ice-cold soda orange and ain't nothin better when you feel sickish. Slim said "We can sit up front now because we crossed the Mason Dixie line," and I axed him what that was, and he said it was the line of the law for *Jim Crow*, and when I axed him who Jim Crow was, he said "That's you, boy."

"I ain't no Jim Crow anyhow," I told him, "'case you know my name is Pictorial Jackson."

"Oh," says Slim, "is that so? Well, I never knowed that, uh-huh. Looky-here Jim," he said, "don't you know about the law that says you can't sit in the front of the bus when the bus runs below the Mason Dixie line?"

"What for you call me Jim?"

"Now Jim!" he says, and cluck-cluck at me solemn. "You mean to tell me you don't know about that line?"

"What line?" I say. "I ain't seed no such a line."

"What?" he say. "Why, we just crossed it back there in Maryland. Didn't you see Mason and Dixie holdin that line across the road?"

"Well," I says, "did we run over it or underneath it?" and I'se tryin to recollect such a thing but jess cain't. "Well," I say, "I guess I musta been sleepin then."

And Slim laugh, and push my hair, and slap his knee. "Jim, you kill me!"

"What did that line look like?" I axed him, 'case I wasn't old enough to know it was a joke yet, you see. Well, Slim said he didn't know what such a line looked like neither on account he never seed it any more than I did.

"But there *is* such a line, only thing is, it ain't on the *ground*, and it ain't in the air neither, it's jess in the head of Mason and Dixie, jess like all other lines, border lines, state lines, parallel thirty-eight lines and iron Europe curtain lines is all jess 'maginary lines in people's heads and don't have nothin to do with the ground."

Grandpa, Slim said that jess as quiet, and didn't call me Jim no more, and said to hisself "Yes sir, that's all it is."

The busdriver man come back, and said "All aboard for NEW YORK" and like I tell you 'bout *travelin* and not goin backwards, we jess went *forwards.* Whoo! Straight ahead was that New York road, and all the traffic of the cars cuttin in and out, zoom, zip, but that driver man jess sit at that wheel 'thout movin a muscle and look right ahead and push his big machine straight on thu as fast as he can go. Anybody come out of a side street and see us comin, why they jess freeze right up and let us come by. That bus man jess cleared the way for hisself, *he* don't care. The others don't care neither 'case they jess barely miss us and go zip thisaway and zip thataway after they miss. I reckon his bus couldn't *ever* stop if somebody got dead in the way, and then you couldn't find their pieces if he did, and couldn't look for the pieces except in the next county. Grandpa, you never seed such drivin and breezin along and ever'body so nonchalant about it, and so sure. I tell you, I couldn't look.

Slim, he was asleep again and this time his head dropped on my arm jess like mine done on his arm in Washington, and slept like that with his eyes closed right in front of the window and here's that bus man carryin him on thu all that road jess as faithful as you please. Slim wasn't scairt none, nor flinched awake or asleep. Well, I shore did love him a whole lot jess then, and said to myself, "Pic, you had no call bein scairt last night when he come and carried you thu the woods and told you not to worry. Now, Pic, you gotsa grow up this minute for Slim. You ain't no country boy *now*."

So I look straight ahead thu the window, and there we go north to NEW YORK in that tremenjous bus.

9. FIRST NIGHT IN NEW YORK

NOW I GOTSA TELL YOU 'BOUT EVER'THING happened in New York and how it happened so fast I jess barely had time to see what New York was like. You see, we come in I believe May 29th to stay and three days later we was all balled up and got to go on the road again, so you see how quick people has to live up in New York and how we was.

When I seed New York was from that bus, and Slim poked me up from the seat and said "Here we are in New York" and I looked and the sun was *red* all over, I looked again, and rubbed my eyes to wake up, for grandpa, we was goin over a long big bridge at run over a whole sight of rooftops and all I has to do is look down to see the chillun runnin betwixt the houses below, Slim said it wasn't New York yet, jess the HOBOKEN SKYWAY

he said, and pointed up ahead to show me New York.
Well I jess could barely see a whole heap of walls and
lanky steeples way, way off yonder all cloudy inside the
smoke. Then I looked all round, and grandpa, it was the
most monstrous and tremenjous stretch of rooftops and
streets, and bridges and railroads, and boats and water,
and great big things Slim said was *gas tanks*, and walls,
and junkyards, and power lines, and in the middle of it
set this old swamp 'at's got tall green grass and yaller
oil in the water, and rusty rafts long the shore. It was a
sight like I never dreamed to see. And here come more
of it where we turn the bridge, and ever'thing's so smoky
and tremenjous, and so laid-out far I can't watch at some
least littlest point of it without I see some more heaped
up yonder behind it in the fog and smoke. Well grandpa,
and that ain't all:—I told you the sun was red, and that
was 'case jess then the sun was peekin thu a big hole in
the clouds up in Heaven, and was sendin down great long
sun-fingers ever'whichway from the hole, and it was all
jess so rosy and purty like if'n God come down thu the
smoke to see the world. Well jess before I woked up I
guess ever'body in New York done put on they lights,
and I guess it was dark then, on account now all them
lights they put on was caught feeble and strange in the red
sunlight and ever'where I look was them po lights burnin
up 'lectricity for nothin, deep inside the streets and the

alleys, up on the walls, up on top the bridges, thisaway in the awful fog and thataway on the soft rosy water, and they jess tremble and shake jess like ever'thing's a big old campfire folks done lit before sundown and didn't dass put it out yet, 'case they knowed it wasn't no real day for long. Well, next thing you know, the sun turn purple and blue and leave jess one peel of fire on the cloudbank, and it gets almost dark.

Slim say, "Ah me it's May again. Wish't I could go someplace tonight," and I say "Ain't we goin no place?"

And he say, "I mean *someplace* where all the boys and girls have their fun. Ain't never seen nor found such a place all my born days. It's what them boys is thinkin 'bout right now."

"What boys is that?" I say, and he point to New York and say "The boys in the jailhouse tonight." Grandpa, I axed him last time if he was in the jailhouse in New York and he said yes, he was *busted* one time but he didn't do nothin wrong, his friend did. He said his friend was in that jailhouse still, and wasn't no better than him.

Well, now I told you how fearsome and grand New York was when I first seed it, and that ain't all. The bus come down into a tunnel and whoosh! it and ever'body else go barrelin along the walls, and it warn't dark in there but *bright* as you like and all lit-up jolly. "Now we's under the Hudson River," brother say, "and wouldn't it be something if that river bust thu and come down on our heads?" I didn't dass guess 'bout that till we come out the other side, and when we did I plum forgot to guess, and I reckon most folks is like that, ain't they grandpa, till the day such a thing happen to them? The bus come out that LINCOLN TUNNEL it was called, and a great yaller light shine up the front of it, and ain't nobody but one man walkin on the street, and I look at him and he look at me too. Well, I guess that man said to hisself "There's a little boy comin to New York for the first time and cain't do nothin but gawk at a man like me 'at's so busy in New York and got so many things to do."

And here we was in New York, and it didn't look half grand now we was inside it on account you couldn't see far with all them *walls* risin clear up on every side. Well you know, I look straight up oncet and I look again and don't see but the most p'culiar brown air in the sky above the tall walls, and I seed it was on account all the lights of New York paint-up the nighttime way high yonder, and do it so much it don't need no more'n a few feeble stars in it. "Them's skyscrapers," Slim said when he seed me look up. Well then the bus turn on a big street, Slim said it was Thirty Four street then I seed plenty far and a whole great gang of folks and grandpa it was jess so many lights strung out one after 'nother, and up, and down, and trembly along the walls, and red, and blue, and all the folks and the car traffic acting jess like ants as far as your eye can see. Grandpa, all the folks you do see, and things they do, and all the streets you do see, and the places there is, and whilst you gotsa keep in mind all the folks and streets you don't see, at's round the corner and way yonder ever'whichaway, and *up* in the skyscrapers, and *down* in the subway — well, you can see how t'ain't pos'ble to make a body unnerstand it lessen they done come and looked for theirselves.

The bus stop, and me and Slim got off and went down the street to the *subway*, which is a tunnel train there underneath New York at ever'body takes to git where they's goin the fastenest best way. "Bus is fast in the country but's too slowed-up in *this* town," Slim say. We pay the man when we pay the gate-machine, and get on the train when the door-machine bring the door open, and get inside and set and let the train-machine run along the rail. Wasn't nobody around to run the doggone thing 'case I looked up front and wasn't nobody steerin it. And I *knowed* we went fast and I wasn't fooled by no dark.

Brother and me got off at Hundred Twenty Five street in *Harlem.*

"We's just around the corner from home, old-timer," Slim say to me, "so you see we made it after all." Well then we come upstairs on the street and it's all as jolly and brightly as Thirty Four street, and grandpa, here we was a *hunnerd* streets up along the city, so you can see how New York never gets to be near the country as you go along it.

"Stand right still whilst I wash your face for Sheila," Slim said, and he stopt me on the street in front of the water-bubbler and rub off my mouth with his handkerchief and great big crowds of folks walks by and it's a nice warm night again and I shore feels glad we come to New York. "Slim," I say, "I's shore glad I ain't at Aunt Gastonia's no more and won't be scairt neither no more." And I look down the street where we come from and say to myself, "No, North Carolina ain't round here no more."

"Well thass the way to talk, soldier," Slim say, "and just because ever'thing's so fine I'm gonta buy Sheila a little thing in the store here so's we'll all have a fine time our first night home."

And we go into a *record store* at's full of men fishin through the record racks and jumpin up and down while they do so like they jess can't wait. Ain't nothin but music and noise in there, and a whole bunch of men out front jumpin jess the same way. Whoo, what fun! Slim, he went fishin and jumpin like ever'body else, and come up with a record, and yelled "Whee! Look what I found!" and ran to the man and throwed him a dollar. Then we go around the corner to a street at wasn't so bright but jess as gay and full of folks in the dark, and run upstairs into a old crumbly hallway, and knock on the door and push it in.

Well, there was Sheila, and I liked her jess as quick as I laid my eyes on her. She was a slim purty gal 'at wore glasses with red horn rims, and a purty red sweater, and purty green skirt, and fine jigglets on her wrists, and when we come in she was standin at the stove makin coffee and readin the paper all at the same time, and looked at us s'prised.

"Baby!" Slim yelled out, and run up and hugged her, and spun her round, and kissed her smack upon the mouth, and said "Looky yonder your new son, mother dear, ain't he somethin fine?"

"Is that Pic?" she said, and come over and took both my hands, and lookt at me down in the eye. "I can see you've been havin lots of trouble lately haven't you, little boy," she said, and I don't know how she could tell that, but she did, and I tried to smile to show I liked for her to be so nice but I was jess a little too bashful. "Well won't you smile sometime?" she said, and I had to go freeze there so foolish and said but jess "Uh-huh" and look away. Doggone it!

Then she said "Wasn't that chile cold comin up here in that little sweater full of holes? And look at his socks, they're full of holes too. Even his poor pants in the back here."

"My hat too," I said, and showed her my hole-hat.

Well, I caught her then and it was her 'at didn't know whether to laugh or look awful, and she got red and laughed. I reckon, grandpa, it was because a boy like me ain't got no call talkin about himself when a lady's doin that for him, ain't it? Well, she was the finest soul, and I knowed it jess then by the way she got red and didn't mind.

Slim said "I'll buy him clothes first thing in the mornin," and Sheila said "How you gonna do that without money?" but he jess started that new record on the record machine in the corner and you shoulda seen him clap his hands and walk up and down with his feet right where he was, and shake his head and say "Oh where's my horn tonight? Oh where's my horn tonight?" over and over, and look up and laugh, 'case he likes the music so much, and say "Play that thing *Slop*jaw!" Grandpa, that record was by Slopjaw Jones done with a saxophone horn and everybody yellin and bangin the piano behind him, and you never heard such reckless jumpin and crashin in your ears out there in the country. Seem like the folks up in the city wants to have fun and ain't got time for no worry exceptin when worry catches up with them, that's when they ain't busy about worryin.

"What do you mean no money?" Slim said, and Sheila said, "I don't like to tell you and Slopjaw, and everybody, and Pic here, but I went and lost my job day before yesterday because they're tearin down the building where the restaurant was down on Madison avenue and puttin up a new office building."

"Office building?" Slim yelled. "Did you say *office* building? What's they goin to do with a *office* building? Ain't nobody get to *eat* in no office building."

"You talk silly," Sheila said, and look at him sad. "Why shoo, all they've got to do is go round the corner to eat in a restaurant."

"Then they put up another office building *there* and then where do you go?" said Slim, and then heaved a sigh. "Doggone it, what are we goin to do now?" He turned off the record, and looked round the kitchen, and began walkin up and down in it, and worried himself to death. I seed then how Slim had worried before about a lots of things. His face dragged down awesome and his eyes jess went starin straight ahead and his bones of his face stuck out from his cheeks and made him look old. Poor Slim, I never forget *that* look on his face when I think about him now. "Dog-*gone*," he jess say, over and over, "dog-*gone*." Then he look at Sheila and she didn't

know it but his face flinch a little bit like if they was
pain way down deep in his heart, and he come back to
say "Dog-*gone!*" and be starin straight ahead after that,
and for a long awesome time. Lord, Lord, Slim always
tried so hard to explain to me and ever'body else the
things on his mind, like he done then. "Dog-gone it,
are we goin to be beat all the time or *ever* make a livin
around here? When will our troubles end? I'm tired
of bein poor. My wife is tired of bein poor. I guess the
world is tired of bein poor, because *I'm* tired of bein
poor. Lord a mercy who's got some money? I know *I*
ain't got some money and that's for sure, now look" and
show his empty pocket.

"You shouldn't of bought that record," Sheila said.

"Well," he said, "I didn't know then. Now so where'd
this money go that folks is supposed to live on? I'd jess
be satisfied if I had a field of my own I could jess grow
things in and wouldn't need no money, and wouldn't
worry *what* folks had it, not records neither. But I ain't
got a field and I need money to eat. Well where am I goin
to get this money? I gotsa get a job. Yes, a job, gotsa get,
I-got-a-git-a-job. Sheila," he call out, "first thing in the
mornin I am goin out and find me a job. You know how
I'm sure I can get one? Because I need one. You know
why I need a job? Because I ain't got no money." And
he went on like that, and got hisself all 'volved in talk,

and come round again to worry some more. "Sheila, I shore hope I get a job tomorrow."

"Well," Sheila said, "I'll have to look for one too."

"It's so hard to get a job that you can't stick to all your life," Slim said. "I wish I could get a job playin tenor in a club and make my livin that way, and express myself with that horn. Show ever'body how I feel by the way I play, and make them see how happy I can be and ever'body can be. Make them learn how to enjoy life and do good in life and unnerstand the world. A whole lot of things. Play sometimes about God, by the way I can make my horn pray in the blues and get down on my knees to signify. Play in such a way as to show ever'body how hard a man tries all the time, and make somebody learn *that*. I want to be like a schoolteacher with that horn, or like a preacher, but show ever'body that jess a musician can do so simple a thing as take a horn in his hand, and blow in it, and finger the stops, yet be a preacher and a schoolteacher in the *result* of what he's doin. I tear my heart out wherever I go. All over this country I've been, and ain't been liked because I was colored, by people who don't mind their own personal business, and don't want me to do good, but I've tore my heart out with that horn. That horn is the only way people come to listen to me. They won't talk on the street, but they'll clap and yell hooray when I'm on the bandstand, and smile at me. Well I smile back, I ain't cool about people, nor cool about nothin. I like to respond and listen and be with people. I feel good most of the time, and do it. Lord a mercy, I sure wantsa live and have my place in the world like they call it and I'm ready to work if I can only work with my horn, because that's the way I like to work and I don't know how to run a machine. Well, I ain't learned yet anyway, and like my horn better, I do. Ar-tist, I'm a ar-tist, jess like Mehoodi Lewin and the columnist in the paper and whoozit. I got a million ideas and can shore pour them out of that horn, and I ain't doin so bad pourin them without the horn. Sheila," he say to her, "less eat some supper and worry about ever'thing tomorrow. I'm hungry and want my strength back. Throw some beans in there, and after supper make a lunch for tomorrow noontime."

"I'll have to make one for myself," Sheila said, and then they wondered what was to happen to me tomorrow, and Slim decided for me to go with him to look for work and we could eat the lunch together. "Make it a big one. You got *bread*? Throw somethin between that bread and that'll be fine. Wished we had a coffee mug. You got a coffee mug? Thermidor you say? Well, *thermidor* it shall be, with the coffee hot. Pic," he said to me, "you and me ain't even started travelin together is we? We just come four and fifty miles and here we go again. Eat, then we go to sleep and get up early. Got a nice old sweater of mine for you tomorrow, and clean socks. Well, we'll make it again. Here we go. Ladies and gentlemen, look out. *Look out for your boy!*" he shouted, and closed his eyes a minute, and stood like that.

Well, that was the first night in New York, and shore 'joyed the supper, and us sittin round the table till ten at night, talkin and recollectin and Sheila told about when she was my age in *Brooklyn,* and all such fine things went on of gabbin together in the nighttime, and me lookin forward to what happen next ever'time I look out the window at New York. I say to myself, "Pic, you left home and come into *New York!*"

I had me a fine cot-bed to sleep on all night.

But that next day wasn't so pleasin as this first night.

10. HOW SLIM LOST
TWO JOBS IN ONE DAY

I'LL NEVER FORGET THAT DAY because so many things happened all at oncet. Started off, me and Slim got up jess as the sun come back red, and he cooked up some eggs and breakfast so's Sheila could sleep some more. Grandpa, ain't nothin better in the world like eggs and breakfast in the mornin because your taster ain't worked all night and ever'thing comes so chawy and smells so fryin good it makes a body wish he could eat ever'body's breakfast all up and down the street seven times, ain't it the truth? When we come down on the street and I seed all them men eatin more eggs and breakfast in the corner store I wished I could eat all the breakfasts in *New York City.* It was a cool mornin and wasn't but six o'clock. I had my new socks, and Slim's black sweater, and Sheila done sewed up the holes in my pants, and I was all set. And you know the first thing happened? We was standin in the doorway and Slim was readin the newspaper *want ads*, and it was mighty chill, and keen, and ever'body come by to get to the work-bus coughin and spittin and shore looked mis'ble from work in New York City, and some of them was readin the papers with the most gloomy disappointed look like if'n the papers complained jess what they hankered to see, and here come a man out of that crowd who knew Slim. "Well there *daddyo*," he said, and showed Slim the palm of his hand, and Slim showed him his, and they touched up like that. "Don't tell me you're lookin for a job again," the man said, and Slim told him he was shore enough.

"Well, I declare, I got a job for you. You know my brother *Henry*. He ain't got up yet this mornin. I jess talked to him. I say *Henry*, ain't you supposed to go to work in that cookie factory down on whatzit street? And he hid under the pillow and says, yes I guess so, uh-huh, but don't move a bone. I say *Henry*, ain't you gettin up? *Henry!* Well now *Henry?* Hey, yoo-hoo, *Henry?* That man just made up his mind to sleep, that's all," and Slim's friend walked off ten feet and come back again.

"Do you think he'll be fired?" Slim axed him curious, and the man said "*Henry?* Will *he* be fired?" Dog my cats if he don't walk off again and come back. "You mean

Henry?" and he looked away, and shook his head, and felt too tired to do anything but hang his head. "Shooee, he's got the *world record* for that. He's been fired more times than he's been hired."

"What's the address of this place?" Slim said, and the man knew it and gave it to us, and made another couple funny jokes and said "Lookout for the boogieman" when me and Slim took off for the job factory. Well, he was all right.

We took the subway, then walked down a street to the river and there was the cookie factory. It was jess a great big old place with chimbleys and lots of machines thunderin inside, and gave out a mighty sweet smell that made us smile. "Why this will be a good job," Slim said, "'cause it smells so good," and we jumped up the steps and come in the office. The boss was there by the punchin clock and was wonderin where was *Henry*, I guess. We waited on a bench a half hour, then the boss said Slim had better start workin all right because nobody was never goin to show up. Slim had to spend some time writin papers, so he told me to wait in the park across the street till noon and then come in for lunch with him. And there he was straight into a job right off quick.

"Sheila'll be happy," I said to myself, and knowed it.

I waited all mornin in that park. It was a tiny park with a iron rail and some bushes, and swings, and such, and jess sat most of the time watchin at a couple other children, and figurin life. I made friends with a little white boy who came into the park with his mother. He was all fine lookin in a blue suit with gold buttons, and knee high stockins, and a red huntin hat. He had a most admirable way of talkin and settin hisself on the bench. His mother read a book on the other bench and smiled at us kindly.

"And why are you waitin here?" he axed me, and I said "My brother works in that factory over yonder."

He says "Why do you say *over yonder*, are you from Texas in the West?"

"*Texas in the West?*" I said. "No, I don't come from up there, I'm from North Carolina." "Are there any cowboys there?" he axed, and I lied and said there was, and we talk. I liked that boy a whole lot. We'd a talked more but he had to go home quick. We was fixin to have a race but he left. Why, he had the goldenest hair and the clearest blue eyes, and I never seed him again.

Well at noon I went up to the factory, and seed Slim by the window with a shovel. All I had to do was sit on a barrel outside the window which was open, and watch Slim till it was time for us to eat.

Well, he was workin so fast he didn't even see me, and when he did, all he had time to do was yell. He bent over with the shovel, and dug into a truckload of fudge, and heaved it up on a belt that rolled around from wheels and carried the fudge clear down the other end of the factory. Before it hit a big roller Slim flatted out the fudge with his hands, then it rolled under and got to be like a sheet of fudge, and then got pieced full of holes by a knife machine 'at jabbed down and made cookies. Slim had to shovel up and then drop the shovel and hurry to use his hands, so's he never could stop one minute because the belt kept turnin. One time he blew his nose and the man down the way said "Send up some more of that chocolate," thass how fast ever'body worked and the rollers rolled. The sweat jess fell from Slim's head and fell in the fudge, and he couldn't do nothin about it, had no time to dry himself. Then a man rolled up another truckload of fudge, only this time it was *vanilla* and all white and purty, and Slim jess stuck that old chocolate shovel in there and hauled it up, all streaky. When he spread the fudge with his hands he looked straight ahead and said "Phew!" because that was the only time he stood up straight enough to talk to himself. That shore was some hard job and I knowed it.

Slim yelled to me "If I stop one second my arms are going to knot up round my neck from Charley Horse!" and jumped back in the fudge. One time he said "Ow!" and one time he said "Whee!" and another time I heard him say "Oh Lord a mercy, I'll never eat a cookie again."

Twelve o'clock, a big whistle blew and all the machines slowed down and ever'body walked off. But Slim, he only leaned there on the post and wiped his head and looked at his hands. Next thing you know, his right hand curled up and reached around for his wrist, and he said it was a *cramp*. Then half of his whole arm curled up like he was showin his muscles, but he wasn't, it was jess another cramp, and he pushed it back and forth and looked at it, and sighed, and cussed.

Well, he came out and we ate the lunch on the office steps in the hot sun. "I hope my arms are better for this afternoon," he said, and was glum and didn't say much more, even when I told him about the little boy I met. Come about one o'clock that big whistle blew again and Slim went back to work.

I watched again. Well, you know, that poor man couldn't grip the shovel when he reached for it, his fingers was so stiff. When he did close his fingers over it his arms began to shake and had no strength in them, and he couldn't hold the shovel at all. The man down the fudge-belt yelled "Start up that vanilla will you? We ain't got all day." Slim called out to the boss and showed him his arms. Both of them stood shakin their heads and thinkin about this, because it *was* sad, and Slim tried again to grip the shovel and couldn't do it, and the boss rubbed his arm some, but Slim jess couldn't control his arms no more. They were red, and hot, and hurt him. Well, he wiped his hands with a rag, and they talked some, then by and by Slim came out the office door and joined me.

"What happened?" I axed him.

"I jess can't work any more today, my arms is tied in a knot." And that's all he said, and we went home with one mornin's pay in a envelope, $3.50.

Sheila came home at five o'clock, and hadn't found a job. Slim told her what happened and we ate supper most silent.

Well, it was the first time I seen Slim gloomy.

"Well I'll tell you," he said after supper, and jess soaked his hands in the hot water, "I don't like them kind of jobs like I had today. I can't shovel fast enough to keep with no rollin belt like that and I used to be a prizefighter too. I don't like to sink my hands in no whole tub of fudge. Do you make your own cookies, gal, or buy it? Shoo, what's I goin to do with a thirty-five-dollar paycheck *any*how when the groceries theirselves cost about twenty, and the rent's took up the rest. I can't be shovelin that doggone stuff up and down myself just so's ever'body can't pay extra bills and can't buy a hat, and my arms get so tired they hang like a broken branch in the tree. I don't want to complain all the time, but shucks almighty no matter how much I love the world and get my kicks every live-long day, and I think Pic here loves the world and gets his innocent joys every day, and you love the world and feel fine in the mornin, it jess ain't the same when there's no dough and the house is black with money debts. It's like a closet you have to sit in, doggone it, 'stead of a house."

"Well, you're just tired today," said Sheila, and she kissed him on the ear and gave him a fine purty sidelook, and trotted off to make coffee on the stove. I reckon Sheila loved Slim like she was his slave. He didn't have to do anything but sit there, and Sheila loved him fine, and watched him, and never passed him in the house without she touched him and sometimes winked at him.

Well, it was mostwise a glum evenin, like you can see, but somethin else happened jess then.

A tall man all well dressed and smilin come in the door, and whoopeed:—"Slim you old tadpole," and ever'body began laughin and forgot their troubles for then. "You know why I'm here, man?" said the man, his name was Charley, and Slim lit up bright and said "You mean?"

"Yes, thass right, a job, and not only that I got a *horn* for you."

"A horn? A horn? My kingdom for a horn! Less go!" and we all went downstairs to the street. Some other man was in the car that had the horn in it, and Slim took the horn out the case and blooped in it a little bit, right on the sidewalk, and felt jess grand. "Where we blow?" he said, and Charley said it was at the Pink Cat Club. "Do

I have to wear a suit?" Charley said he shore did have to because the boss man at the Pink Cat was jess complete persnickity about such things and wouldn't pay Slim no five dollars if he didn't like him.

"Well *hoe-down!* Here we go for five dollars Sheila baby," Slim said, and ran upstairs as fast as he could run to put on his suit. Sheila hurried and put on a nice dress, and brushed *me* up some, and here we was all goin to the Pink Cat Club together not five minutes after Slim had sat so glum and sad. Grandpa, life ain't happy, and then it's happy, and goes on like that till you die, and you don't know why, and can't ask nobody but God, and He don't say nothin, do He? Grandpa, Slim and Sheila was so fine that night I *knowed* God was on their side jess then, and I thanked Him. Ain't I right, grandpa, to pray when I feel grateful and glad like I did then? Well, that's what I done.

The man zipped that car, and ever'body was glad, and it started rainin but nobody paid it mind, and we got to the club real early and set *parked* in front of it a minute whilst Slim and the men had theirselves a smoke and talked. We was still in *Harlem* about thirty streets up along the way, and it still looked like jess where we lived. The rain got on the street and made the purtiest manner of red and green lights, jess like a Arabian Nights and made rainbows. It was a fine rainy night for Slim to start workin inside that club in, and for me and Sheila to hear him. Well we shore had fun in that car. Slim took out the horn again and went *"BAWP"* with it to try out the lowliest note and then tried a run up and down the middle notes, and finished up with a little high *"BEEP"* and ever'body laughed. "Ouch my fingers," Slim said. Those two fellows was fine fellows, Charley and th'other man, 'case they shore admired Slim and watched.

"Only thing, Slim," Charley said, "that suit of yours is a little beat." Slim's suit was his onliest suit, and it was a old blue coat with the whitebelly insides showin out under the arms, and there was a rip in the pants he didn't have time to sew up. Charley said "I know it's the only suit but this Pink Cat joint is s'posed to be a *cocktail lounge,* you know, nobody's satisfied anymore with a regular old saloon."

"Well," Slim laughed, and didn't care, "less go play some music."

And we all went in the Pink Cat Club suit or no suit, on time or early or what-all, you know. Well, it was early. The boss wasn't there yet. The bandstand wasn't lit up. Folks was drinkin at the bar and playin the big *jukebox* machine and talkin low.

Slim ran up the bandstand, and clicked on the light. "Come on Charley, let's have some piano." Charley allowed it was too early and hung back shy, but Slim allowed no such thing and dragged him up there. Charley said the other boys in the band wasn't here yet but it made no difference to Slim. The other man that was with us, he was the drummer, and didn't say nothin, but just sat down behind Slim and knocked the drum and chewed his gum. Well, when Charley seen this he decided to sit down at the piano and play the music too.

Sheila bought me a Coca-Cola and made me sit down in the corner by myself to watch. She stood up right in front of Slim whilst he played his first number and didn't ever move from there till he was finished, and he played the whole first song to her. He blew in the horn, and moved his poor fingers, and I tell you grandpa he made the purtiest deepdown horn-sound like when you hear a big New York City boat way out in the river at night, or like a train, only he made it sing up and down melodious. He made the sound all trembly and sad, and blew so hard his neck shaked all over and the vein popped in his brow, as he carried along the song in front of the piano, and the other man swisht the drum with the broom brushes soft and breezy. And on they went. Slim never took his eye away from Sheila till the middle of the song, then he remembered me and looked across the room and pointed the horn at me and play extra purty to show me how good he could play even though his hands was hurt and he couldn't work in that old cookie factory. Then he turned the horn back to Sheila and finished the song with his head way down on the mouthpiece and the horn against his shoe, and stood like that bowed.

Well you know, ever'body at that bar clapped, and was excited too, and one man said "You blowed that one, son," and I could see they liked Slim better and shut down that *jukebox* by all means.

Sheila come over and sat with me, and there we was, right by the window and could see the purty lights out on the wet street, and see the whole bar and all the folks in front of us, and the bandstand perfect. Now Slim beat down his feet real fast and the drummer man walloped one, and off they went and jumped. Whoo! Slim jess grabbed that horn and hoisted it up and blew with all his might and moved his head from side to side with his jaws workin hard and fast like workin with his hands that day. When I seen that I realized how strong Slim was all over, and made of iron.

Ever'body at the bar jumped when they heard him.

"Yes, yes, yes, yes," yelled that man at the bar and grabbed his hat and hung on to it and stepped up and down in front of ever'body jazzy. He shore could make his feets go, that gen'l'man. Well, he was dancin to Slim.

Slim, he was walkin up and down where he was and jess carryin along that jump-song goin as fast, well, like that *bus* I was tellin you about earlier. He was pushin the horn to go ever' old way zippin here and zoopin there, he then all drawed-out himself on one breath way high up, and threw it way down *"BAWP"* and back again in the middle, and the drummer-man looked up from his crashing sticks and yelled "Go Slim!" jess like that. Charley, he was poundin on the piano with all his fingers spread, *blam,* jess when Slim is catchin his breath, and *blam* again when Slim comes back. Grandpa, Slim had more breath than ten men and could go on all night like that. Wow, I never heard anything like it, and anybody makin some noise and music by himself. Sheila, she jess sat there grinnin at her old Slim and knocked her hands together under the table to the beat of the drum. Well, I done the same thing. I shore wished I could dance right then.

"Go, go, go!" yelled that man with the hat and flipped himself back and pawed at the air with his arms and said "Great-day-in-the-mornin!" jess as loud as a big old fog-horn 'bove the noise. Whee, he was funny.

Well now Slim was startin to sweat because nobody wanted to stop, and he didn't wantsa stop neither and blew right on in that horn till the sweat begun pourin down his face jess like it did over the shovel in the mornin. Oh, he jess watered that bandstand from sweat. He didn't ever run out of anything to play ever'time he crossed from one end of the song to th'other, and had a hunnerd years in him of it. Oh, he was grand. That song lasted twenty minutes and the folks at that bar got out in front of the bandstand and clapped in time for Slim in one great big jumpin gang. I could jess see Slim over their heads with his face all black and wet and like he was cryin and laughin all at the same time, only his eyes was closed and he didn't see them but jess plain knew they was there. He was holdin, and pushin that horn in front of him like it was his *life* he was rasslin with, and jess as solemn about it, and unhappy. And ever' now and then he made it laugh too, and ever'body laughed along with it. Oh, he talked and talked with that thing and told his story all over again, to me, to Sheila and ever'body. He jess had it in his heart what ever'body wanted in *their* hearts and they listened to him for some of it. That crowd rocked under him, it was like the waves and he looked like a man makin a storm in that ocean with his horn. One time he let out a big horselaugh with his horn, and hung on to it when ever'body yelled to hear more, and made all kinds of designs with it till it didn't sound like a horselaugh no more but a mule's *heehaw*. Well, they axed him to hold that but he moved on to a high, long drawed-out whistle that sounded like a dog whistle and pierced into my ears, but after awhile it didn't pierce no more but jess was there like ever'thing was made dizzy like Slim felt from holdin that long note. It made you sympathize before he jumped on down back to reg'lar notes and made ever'body jump and laugh again.

A bunch of new folks come in and Slim seen them and decided to end the song there.

It wasn't time to play yet anyhow. He wiped himself with a towel from the kitchen and we all sat down to-gether in the corner, with Charley and the drummer-man. A man come over from the bar and axed Slim if he ever played with a big band. "Ain't I seen you with Lionel Hampton or Cootie Williams or somebody?" Slim said no, and the man said: "You ought to be with a big band and start makin yourself some money. You don't want to play for peanuts in a place like this all your life, with a taped-up horn. Go down see an agent."

"Agent?" Slim said. "Is that who you see to work with a band?" Slim was s'prised and didn't know any of these things.

Another man come by, and laughed, and shook Slim's hand, and walked back to the bar, jess like that without talkin.

This was how they liked Slim, and what a real fine musician he was.

Well, here come the boss walkin in at nine o'clock, and the rest of the band is with him, includin the leader, who was Charley's older brother, and they all get ready to go on the bandstand. But that big sharped-up boss man seen Slim's tear under his coat and said, "Haven't you got a better suit than that? No? Can't you borrow one from one of these boys?" Ever'body looked at ever'body else, and talked about it, and come to figure there wasn't but one suit they could loan him, only it was down in Baltimore. Well, Baltimore is a long ways off, and the boss had to admit it when he thought about it, but he jess didn't seem to like the idea of Slim in that poor awful suit. He hedged and hawed about it, and began shakin his head after awhile, and I began to see Slim's chance to make five dollars was all ready to go wrong. Slim seen that, and argued with the boss. He said "It don't make no difference, nobody'll see me, looky here I'll hold my arms down" and showed him.

"Well," said that boss, "I know but I'm havin a big holiday crowd tonight and it'll be pretty *toney* as it gets in the later hours, and it just wouldn't look good, don't you see. It's just not, ah, hem, the *thing*." And if you ask me, grandpa, I'd say he wanted to save that five dollars anyhow. One of the boys in the band was sick and Slim was only takin his place, and the boss figured he didn't need nothin or nobody, and didn't.

So out we went, Slim, Sheila and me, to go home, and walked it this time, in the rain. And you know the first thing Slim said?:— "I didn't really get goin on that horn tonight," and that was what he was worried about. Sheila didn't say nothin, but jess held Slim's arm and marched along with him, and enjoyed the walk, and seemed gay.

Well, Slim asked her what she was so gay about, and she told him. You know how poor they was, and the money worries they had that very day, and the rent comin up in a day or two like Slim said. And you know how Slim was always talkin about Californy, and seemed to hint to Sheila about her comin there with him. I didn't tell you, but he come from Californy to marry her before he come to get me, and was out there most of the time since he left North Carolina in his boyhood. Well, Sheila took all that and wrapped it up in one package for Slim, like a Christmas present, and said "Let's use that hundred dollars in my girdle and go to California. I'll tell my mother we have to do it and can't help it. We'll stay at my sister's house in San Francisco to start with. Then we can get jobs, there as well as here I guess. What do you think?"

"Baby," laughed Slim and hugged her, "that's just what I want to do."

And that's how we come to decide to go to Californy, on that day Slim lost two jobs.

11. PACKING FOR CALIFORNY

WE SPENT TWO WHOLE DAYS PACKIN. Sheila's mother lived right around the corner and come to visit us three, four times to argue with Sheila about goin to Californy *cold* like that. Seems Sheila's family lived in New York so long, with such long jobs, they didn't believe in traipsin around the country like that, and once tried to stop Sheila's sister from goin to Californy, that was Zelda, the one we was goin to live with out there. But Slim said, "New York people are always afraid to move from where they are. Californy is the place to be, not New York. Didn't you ever hear that song Californy Here I Come, Open Up That Golden Gate? All that sun, and all that land, and all that fruit, and cheap wine, and crazy people, it don't scare you so much when you can't get a job because then you can always live some way if you even just eat the grapes that fall off the wine trucks on the road. You can't pick no grapes off the ground in *New York,* nor walnuts either."

"Now who's talkin about eatin *grapes* and walnuts?" yelled Sheila's mother. "I'm talkin about a roof over your head." She was a woman of some level sense.

"You don't need one in Californy because it's never cold," said Slim, and laughed in his head gleeful. "Oh, you ain't never seen such nice sunny days when you don't need a *coat* most the year round, and don't have to buy coal to heat your house, or get overshoes or nothin. And you never die of the heat in the summer up north in Frisco and Oakland and thereabouts. I tell you, that's the place to go. Ain't nowhere else to go in the United States and it's the last place on the map—after it, ain't nothin but water and Russia."

"And what's wrong with *New York?*" Sheila's mother snapped up.

"Oh, nothin!" Slim pointed out the window. "Atlantic Ocean is got the Devil for the wind in the wintertime, and the Devil's son carries it down the streets so's a man can freeze to death in a doorway. God brought the sun over Manhattan Island, but the Devil's cousin won't let it in your window unless you get yourself a penthouse a mile high and you don't dass step out of it for a breath of air for fear you'll fall that mile, if you could afford a penthouse. You can go to work, but probably wind up havin two hours left to yourself after a eight-hour day made into twelve hours by subway, bus, elevated, tube, ferry, escalator, and elevator and waitin in between, it's so *big* and hopeless town. Ain't nothin wrong with New York, nope. Go around the corner to see your friend after supper, see if he's there or ten miles downtown wishin he could see you. Try to have a ensemble evenin when your pockets are empty, like any country boy, and the man'll look for a blackjack in your pants."

That's how *he* talked about things.

"Future of the United States was always goin to Californy, and always bouncin back from it, and always will be."

"Well don't come bouncin back on *me* if you go broke out there," said Sheila's mother and said it to Sheila.

"We're broke as it is," Sheila said, and that woman her mother shore didn't like any of it.

Well, I didn't tell you about the money, but there wasn't enough for all three of us to go by bus. Sheila was goin to have her first baby before six months so she had to take sixty dollars of the hunnerd and go by bus and *eat good.* Me and Slim, we had the forty dollars and some more him and Sheila still had, and because rent was due in two days we was movin out, and sendin clothes and dishes in two big old suitcases and a smaller one,

82

by railroad, and then me and Slim, with that $48, was
hitchhikin to the Coast right away, and eat good too but
be *on the bum with our thumbs* and sleep in beds only
part of the time, mostly in cars and trucks and parks in
the afternoon.

It shore sounded good and fine to me. But I didn't
know *then* how far that Californy Coast was.

The last night ever'thing was packed and ready to go
in the mornin and we had coffee in the kitchen and house
looked so bare Slim seemed most gloomy about it. "Look
at this place we've been livin in. We leave it, someone
else comes in, and life is jess a dream. Don't it remind
you of old cold cruel world to look at it? Those floors
and bare walls. Seemed we never lived here, and I never
loved you inside of it."

"We'll make ourselves a new home in Californy," said
Sheila, gladly.

"What I want is a *permanent* home and spend our
lives in one neighborhood, up on a hill till I get old and
grandpa."

"We'll see," said Sheila, "and pretty soon Pic'll have a
little brother in Californy."

"First we've got to go three thousand and two hundred
miles," sighed Slim, and I remembered that later. "Three
thousand and two hundred miles," he said, "over a plain,
a desert and three mountain chains and any and all the

rain that feels like fallin down. Praise the Lord." Well, we went to bed and slept the last night in that house, and sold the beds in the mornin. "Now we're out in the cold," Slim said, and he was right. In the afternoon we left the house dead empty except for a old bottle of milk, and my North Carolina socks too.

Sheila had her suitcase, and me and Slim had one suitcase with all our things in it. Off we went, to the bus station, and bought Sheila's ticket and waited around for her time to go.

By the time her bus was ready we all felt terrible sad and scared. "There I go into the night," Sheila said when she saw that bus that said CHICAGO on it. "I'm goin and I'll never probably come back again. It's jess like dyin to go to Californy—but here I come." Grandpa, I ain't forgot that minute.

"It'll be more like livin when you get there," Slim laughed, and Sheila said she hoped so. "Don't let no boys mess with you on that bus," Slim said, "because you're plumb alone till Pic and me get there, which I don't know when."

"I'll be waitin for you, Slim," and Sheila begun cryin. Well, Slim didn't cry but he looked it when he hugged her. Poor girl—she shore seemed pitiful that night, and I shore loved her plenty, jess like Slim said I would on that first night in the woods. Jess a young mother, and don't know what'll happen to her on the other side of the country, and all that nighttime alone in front of her till Slim and I got there. Jess like the Bible said, A fugitive and a vagabond shalt thou be in the earth, only she was a girl. I reached out and touched her cheek, and told her wait for us in Californy.

"You be extra careful with yourselves hitchhikin," she said. "Still seems to me Pic is too little for such hard travelin, well, and I don't feel right about it."

But Slim said I'd be safe and sound with him, as much as *he* could be by himself, and if he couldn't make it nobody could. This's how Slim felt, and was sure, and watched over us. So him and Sheila kissed, and then she kissed me so soft and sweet, and in the bus she goes.

"Goodbye Sheila," I said, and waved, and felt more so terrible lonesome and scairt than when she cried, and goodbye, goodbye ever'body else was sayin to ever'body else round the bus, and grandpa that's how sad it is to travel and roam, and try to live and go about things, I reckon till the day you die.

So Sheila went, and was gone, and now me and Slim had to catch up with her hitchhikin over that land.

We walked from the bus station to a big lit-up street called Times Square, and Slim said we was goin out the way we come in, at the Lincoln Tunnel, and hoped that old hole would point us to the West and nowhere else when we shot out of it. "First we'll have our Hot Dog Number One on Times Square," he said.

That's what we done, and grandpa I'll never forget that night of Hot Dog Number One on Times Square, jess about an hour it took us to eat it, before we hit that road.

12. TIMES SQUARE AND THE MYSTERY OF TELEVISION

THERE WAS A WHOLE LOT OF MEN STANDIN on the corner of Eighth Avenue and Forty Second in front of a big gray bank that was closed for the night. In the middle of the road it was all tore up from constructin work, and cars bumped by over the rocky sand along the sidewalk. It was a cold night for spring, felt more like autumn weather, and a whole lot of papers blowed by in the wind and the lights shined ever'whichside and flashed in that wind like so many eyes twinklin. It was jolly, and people had to be a wee bit frisky to keep warm, so they jumped about. Me and Slim bought the hot dogs and spread some mustard on em, and strolled over to the corner to see what was goin on while they cooled a minute.

Lord, there was a couple two, three hunnerd men on one side of the street. Most of them was listenin to the speeches of the Salvation Army. Four Salvations took turns makin speeches, and while one was speakin the other three jess stood there like ever'body else lookin up and down the street to see what else was goin on. Here come a tall white-haired man of ninety years old clompin thu the crowd with a pack on his back, and when he seen ever'body listenin to the speeches he raised his right hand and said *"Go moan for man"* as clear and loud as a foghorn in the wind, and clomped right on by like he hadn't a minute to stop awhile. "Where you goin Pop?" a man said in the crowd, and the old man yelled it back over his head—*"California* my boy"—and he was gone around the corner with that white hair flowin.

"Well," said Slim, "he's not lyin and that's the tunnel he's headed for."

Then here come a loud siren motorcycle, and then another, and a third, all screechin together and escortin the way thu the traffic fo a big black limousine with a spotlight on it. All the men on the corner stooped down to see who was in that car. Me and Slim coulda reached out and touched it and made it a sign, it was so close. The limousine slowed in the sand, and started again, and a man in the crowd yelled "Look out for that Arkansas clay" and some of the men laughed because here it was

New York clay and not much of it. Well, wasn't nobody inside the limousine except two, three men with hats on, you know.

Then, grandpa, the word come floatin by in the heaven and I was so scairt, I'd never seen no such thing in all my born days like a word floatin by in the heaven, but Slim said it was jess a old balloon with a electric sign on it nudgin down close to Times Square for ever'body to see. Well, a couple folks looked up and didn't look s'prised, and I *knowed* these New Yorkers was ready and used to ever'thing. It was a purty balloon, and hovered around the longest time, and had to fight with the wind, but tacked and rassled right up there for Times Square. Not so many folks was lookin at it, a shame, bein such a purty balloon like that. Well, my cousins back in Carolina would appreciate it shore a lot. I know I did. It turned its nose into the wind, and wobbled, and jess floated back like a breeze and turned its nose around again and had to buck on back. It was best when it missed and ballooned. I couldn't hear what the poor thing sounded like there was so much fuss below.

A number of things like this was goin on, and those Salvation Army speechers howled right along in the noise and roar. The Lord *this* and the Lord *that* is all they kept sayin, and I don't remember exactly, except about *burning in the fires of repentance* and them talkin to ever'body like they was sinners. Well, maybe ever'body do be sinners but it ain't innerestin on the street corner to hear it challenged, 'case there ain't nobody likely to step up and confess all his sins in front of the police-man that's always teeterin on his heels right there. What's I goin to explain to the police-man about the fire I started in Mr. Otis' cornfield that cost him twenty dollars of feed and nobody ever knowed it was me. Well, no New York man that lives right there is goin to step up and tell how he threw his cigarette away and burned down the hospital in his block, and any such thing. Besides of which, why don't the speechers go into detail about *their* own sins they keep repentin and folks could work from there and judge. But it grew innerestin when a new man stepped up on the other side of the corner and started a speech of his own. He had a much louder voice and drew a bigger crowd. And it was the shabbiest crowd drew about *him.* He was jess a ordinary lookin man in a black hat, with shiny eyes.

"Ladies and gentlemen of the world, I have come to tell you about the mystery of television. Television is a great big long arm of light that reaches clear into your front parlor, and even in the middle of the night when there ain't no shows going on that light is on, though the studio is dark. Study this light. It will hurt you at first, and bombard your eyes with a hundred trillion electronic particles of itself, but after awhile you won't mind it no more. Why?" he yelled way up loud and Slim said "Yes!" The man said, "Because while electricity was light to see by, *this* is the light comes not to see by, but to *see* — not to read by, but to *read*. This is the light that you *feel*. It is the first time in the world that light has been gathered up from the sources of light and shot through a tube in a way that it can be watched and studied instead of blinked at. And it has taken the shape of men and women who are real flesh and blood at the studio but come streaming into your parlor in *light* with all their sounds shot in sidetrack. What does this mean, ladies and gentlemen?"

Well, nobody knowed that, and waited, and Slim said "Go, man!" and to hear it.

"It means that man has discovered light and is fiddling with it for the first time, and has released concentrated shots of it into everyone's house, and nobody yet knows what the effect will be on the mind and soul of people, except that now there is a general feeling of nervousness among some, and sore eyes, and twitching of nerves, and a suspicion that because it has come at the same time as the A T O M there may be an unholy alliance betwixt one and the other, and both are bad and injurious and leading to the end of the world, though some optimists claim it is the opposite of the atom and may relax the nerves the atoms undid. Nobody knows!" he moaned way out loud, and looked at ever'body frank. Well, ever'body was innerested and paid no attention to the speeches about *repentance*, and Slim agreed, most amazed.

"And ladies and gentlemen," he said, "it is the old-time Depression traveling salesman that used to put his foot in your door and now has got a leg in your parlor, except he looks so doggone strange in light you just can't believe his transformation. And don't think *he* ain't more nervous than the Depression days jiggling behind all that light and looking out into the unknown America. Yes ladies and gentlemen and I seen a salesman on television last night who put on a mask for fun and yet his eyes looked awfully scared peeking from behind that mask at a million other better-hidden eyes. What does this mean?" he demanded, and ever'body was ready to kneel to find out, so to speak, and Slim yelled "Go!" and socked his hands together.

"The day shall come when one giant brain shall televize the Second Coming in light and everyone in the world shall see it in their brains by means of a brain-television that Christ Himself shall cause to be switched on in a miracle and no one shall be spared from knowing the Truth, and everyone shall be saved forever, and men and women of the world I warn you, live as best as you can and be hereinafter kind to one another and that is all there is to do now. We all know this." And off he trots

Pic

jess as calm as you please, and Slim looked after him with the most satisfied and glad look and clapped his hands, so that a whole bunch of others clapped their hands too, and the speecher vanished in glory. Grandpa, it was as strange as that.

Then the Salvation Army man howled out at us "Don't you realize the Lord is coming?" and jess then a loud screechin and crashin come down the street flamin red lights ever'whichway and I ducked, it was the fire engines barrelin to a fire with a whole bunch of firemen hangin on to their hats most solemn and displeased, and goin a hunnerd miles a hour. Whoo! that roused us, and Slim said "Whee!" and ever'body shore looked amazed and innerested then ever'thing got back to normal and people slouched around bored like always.

Well, it was time to go, and Slim said, "We'll come back to Times Square sometime, but now we gotsa go across that night, like the old man with the white hair, and keep goin till we get on the other side of this big, bulgin United States of America and all the raw land on it, before we be safe and sound by the Pacific Sea to set down and thank the Lord. Are you ready Pic?" he said, and I said "Yes," and off we go.

13. THE GHOST OF THE SUSQUEHANNA

IT WAS EIGHT O'CLOCK when we went and stood in front of the Lincoln Tunnel in all that yaller light, and it started mistin jess a little, enough to worry me and Slim even before we was begun on the road. But for the first time since that time, we got a ride inside a minute; seemed like the man at the wheel come around the corner sayin "pleased to meet you" before we could even show our thumbs. He lit up with a smile and throwed open the door. It was a big gigantic yaller truck that said PENSCO on it, with a tractor-cab in front a good twelve feet high, and the biggest tires in the world, and hauled a trailer you couldn't see over of without backin up across the street. A mighty gigantic thing, that Slim had to throw me up to get in, and the man cotch me like a football. When I sat up there it felt like bein in a tree, it was so grand and high. Slim jumped after, and hauled in that suitcase that had all our clothes, and here we go.

"Going someplace with your kid brother?" the driver said. "It don't do for him to get caught in the rain," and with that he kicked down, and grabbed two clutches, and socked ever'thing around and pumped his feet like an organ-player, and boom! that big truck started to roll and growl, and bowled down into the tunnel like a mountain. It was a white man drivin it. His name was Noridews. And he made that tunnel shake and reverberate from there to New Jersey.

Not only that he didn't say another word till we got to Pennsylvania hours later, and all Slim and me had to do was sit and enjoy the way he throwed that gigantic machine down the highway. He was ever so much stronger than a poor *bus*, and that is a heap of strength. People in the other cars seemed to quake and wobble when we come by spit-boom eatin up ever'thing in sight. Only time he stopped was on a hill, and only stopped *passin* people then, didn't stop rollin at all. He had the mightiest brakes in the world to stop that trailer bumpin us down the back at ever' red light, and had to kick for his life on the brakes they handled such powerful stops and was so supple. Then the trailer bucked to a stop, like a mule, and edged along like it couldn't wait too long at no red light, and the driver told it to hold fast but it edged along no lesser. "She's got to go," he said.

Well, the mist was rainin in New Jersey, and grandpa, the first thing Slim and I seen was that old white man with the silver hair flowin around his head, walkin along in the highway in all that yaller light with the rain blowin over him like the smoke. Oh, he looked pitiful and grand all at the same time for an old man. Slim said, "He got a poor short ride from New York." We looked at him when we boomed by, and seen his face stuck out in the rain and him deep in thought of somethin like it never rained and like he wasn't anywhere but in his room, you know. "What's he goin to do?" Slim said, and "Oh that wonderful gentleman he puts me in the mind of Jesus, trackin along like that in this dismal world. I bet he don't pay no taxes, neither, and his toothbrush was lost in Hoover's Army. Ah," he said, "ever'body's bound to make it at the same time if *he* ever makes it." The old man had the bluest eyes, I seen that when we rolled by. Seen him later, tell you when some day.

We rolled through all the crowded streets of New Jersey, and got on the road, and come to a sign that said "South" with an arrow pointin flat to the left, and "West" with an arrow pointin straight down, and stayed right on the straight arrow down into the West. It got dark, and countrylike, and pretty soon there was hills.

It took some hours to get to Pennsylvania where the man was drivin to, and about five to get to Harrisburg, Pennsylvania, where he lived. I slept some of the way. It kept right on rainin. Inside the cab was warm and comfortable, and a good start it was for me and Slim. He said he wasn't far behind Sheila after all.

At Harrisburg at midnight the man said he could save time by droppin us off outside town at a junction and pointed to it when we passed, and it was a lonely rainy junction that made me gulp it was so dark, but he said he would take us in anyhow to make sure we connected right for Pittsburgh and points west, and added he knowed another short cut downtown. That was good for us, that short cut. Harrisburg was all lit up in halos in the rain and looked quiet and gloomy. There was big gray bridges, and the Susquehanna river below them, and the main street in town where ever'body was waitin for buses at midnight.

Me and Slim jumped out of the tractor-cab at the red light, and the man repeated his instructions over whilst Slim thanked him gladly, and then back we was on foot, goin slant across town for the other highway with hopes on high. "That was a good ride," Slim said, "and I wouldn't of got one like it alone. Ever'body'll sympathize with you bein so little and we'll make time to the Coast. Pic, you're my goodluck chile. Come along with me you old daddyo."

The houses in Harrisburg is extremely old, and come from the time of George Washington, Slim said. They's all old brick in one part of town, and have crooked chimbleys and ancient shapes but look all neat. Slim said the town was so old because it was on a great old river. "Ain't you ever heard of the Susquehanna, and Daniel Boone and Benjamin Franklin and the French and Italian wars? In those times ever'body was here, and come from New York where we was, with pushcarts and oxes over the hills that truck groaned on, in rain and high weather, and suffered and died jess to reach it here. It was the beginnin of the big long push to California and now you remember how long it took us to get here by truck then figure it by ox, and *then* tell me about it when we get to San Francisco—about the ox. I'll ask you about it when we go over the sink in Nevady. In Nevady they's a sink that took down a *whole ocean* and's been dry ever since, and takes a month to measure the edges of it. Ain't nobody wash their teeth over that sink. You ain't seen nothin yet, boy."

Well, we was still in Susquehanna and hungry enough to be in Nevady, so Slim said we'd have Hot Dog Number Two and Hot Dog Number Three and maybe Four. We went to a diner and ate them, and had a side dish of beans with katchup, and coffee both of us. Slim said I had to learn to drink coffee to keep warm on the road.

He counted his money, said we had $46.80 left, and dug down in the suitcase to put on more clothes in case it rained bigger. He said he hoped we got a ride soon so's I could sleep, and wished I could wake up in Pittsburgh and then we'd move right on 'stead of sleepin. "Up ahead the sun is shinin in Illinois and Missouri, I *know* it," he said.

By and by we hit the night again, and Slim brought along two packs of cigarettes that left us $46.40, and we walked to the outskirts of town. Folks looked at us curious and wondered what we was doin. Well, that's life. *A man's got to live and get there*, Slim always said about that. "Life is a sneeze, life is a breeze," he said. Along come a car with a man goin home from work and Slim didn't care, he threw out his thumb and whistled 'most shrill through his teeth, and when he seen the man wouldn't stop, why he stuck his leg and pulled up the pants and said "Have pity on a poor young girl of the road." Tickled me the way he fooled around ever'where he went.

It was cold, and it *was* raw, but we felt real fine jess like we was home. Ever' now and then I got to worryin about findin a bed and home in Californy, and worried about Sheila, and worried about gettin tireder than I was, and damper, in a darker place than this, but Slim made me forget it the way he went along. "It's the only way to live," Slim said, "jess don't die. Whoopee, sometimes I feel like dyin but now I wantsa wait the *longest* time. Bein that you bring it in some more, Lord, I ain't afraid of a few cold toes so long's my whole foot don't crack. Lord, you didn't give me any money but you gave me the right to *complain.* Whoo! Complain so long on the left hand, the other hand'll fall off. Well, I've got my baby, I'll hold on jess a while longer, and see what Californy looks like now, and look around inside myself, and bet. I can't do no more than *kick*, Lord, kick this way, kick that way, and then I kick it proper. Look out for you boy, Lord." Slim was always talkin to God like that. We got to know each other fine and could talk to ourselves anytime, the other one only listened. I'd say "Tick, tack, toe!" countin my footsteps and Slim would say "There you go!" jess as absent-minded and thinkin about somethin else. It was the grandest fun, and good.

Someday grandpa I'll make a whole lot of money for you and me, but I'll enjoy it like Slim enjoyed it *without* no money, and make sure to be a happy man.

We crossed over the town, and pretty soon there we was on the highway and there was the Susquehanna River runnin right with us, most solemn and black and not makin a sound for miles.

And here come a man with a little tiny suitcase hurryin along most jaunty from the shore, and seen us, and waved, and said "Walk a little faster if you want to keep up with me, for I'm goin to CANADY and I don't aim to waste time." Well, he wasn't even caught up with us and talked like that, but soon enough he passed us. "Can't lag, son, can't lag," he said, and was lookin back. Me and Slim hurried on after him quick.

"Where you headed?" Slim said, and the man—he was jess a little old man, white, and poor—said "Why, I'm gonna get me a HIBALL up the river here soon's I cross the bridge. Member of the Veterans of Foreign Wars and the American Legion. Red Cross in this town wouldn't give me a dime. Tried to sleep in the railyards last night and they put a spotlight on me. Told them 'You'll never see me in *this* town again,' walked away. Had a good breakfast last week, Martinsburg, West Virginia, pancakes, syrup, ham, toast, two glasses milk and a half, and a Mars candy bar. Always like to load up for the winter like a squirrel. Had grits and brains in Hippensburg two weeks now, and wasn't hungry for three days."

"You mean Harrisburg?"

"Hippensburg, son, Hippensburg, Pennsylvania. I've got to meet my pardner in Canady by month's end so I can go into a uranium deal. Know upstate New York!" he said wavin his fist most determined. He was a funny old man, was short and thin, all weazled up his face that had such a long horny nose, and looked so shrunk and wan under his hat I wouldn't recognize if I seen him again. "Walk fast," he yelled to usn's behind, "knew a boy three years ago on this road jess the same as you. Lazy! Slow! Don't lag!" We followed him and had to hustle some.

We walked about two mile.

"Where we goin?" Slim said.

"Know what I had me in Harrisburg last night? One fine meal I tell you, in any diner in the world. Had candied pig's feet, yams, with peas, peanut butter sandwich and two cups tea and Jello with fruits in it. Old Veteran of Foreign Wars cook behind the counter. On the twelfth of this month had me a cold shower followed by hot, in the Cameo Hotel, won't tell you where, desk clerk was Jim, Veteran of Foreign Wars, I caught a cold and sneezed myself all over."

"You sure keep movin along, Pop," said Slim.

"Old silver-haired man with a pack an hour ago couldn't even keep up with me. All set for Canady, I am. Got things in this bag. Got a nice new necktie, too." His bag was a poor little tore-up piece of cardboard and was held together by a big belt tied around it. He kept fiddlin at the belt. "Wait a secont while I take out that tie," he said, and we all stopped in front of a empty gas station and he kneeled down to undo the belt.

I sat down and caught back the rest in my legs, and watched. That man was so funny, that was why Slim was followin him and talkin to him so. Slim jess went along trailin what innerested him, you know, and couldn't say no to any old man like that.

"Now where can that tie be?" said the old man, and fiddle-faddled around in his busted satchel the longest time, and scratched his haid. "Now don't tell me I left it in Martinsburg. I packed two dozen cough drops that morning and remember the tie was stuck up alongside. No it wasn't Martinsburg at all, at all, at all, now where was it? Harrisburg? Ah shoot, this old tie will do till I get to Ogdensburg, New York State," and off we went again walkin. He didn't have no such a tie.

Grandpa don't believe it if you will, but we walked SIX more miles along that river with that old man, and somethin was supposed to be around the bend ever' time, but there never was anything. I never walked so much and minded it so little, he talked so crazy. "I have all my papers," he kept sayin, and told us what he done in ever' town for the past month to eat, how he showed his cridentials at places, and what the meal was, and how much sugar he put in his coffee and crackers in his soup. It made me and Slim hungry to hear him. He's so small, and loved food so large. And walked, and walked.

Well, that somethin never showed up and we had walked clear into the wilderness where the road lit in only the longest spaces.

Slim stopped cold, and said "Say, you must be . . ."
but didn't wanta say "crazy" and just said "You must
be . . . Pop, me and my brother better turn back."

"Back? No back about this part of the country. Heh
heh. I just misjudged you boys like I misjudged that
young man three years ago, that's all I done. I'm ready
to go on if you ain't."

"Well, we can't walk all night," Slim said.

"Go ahead, give up, I'm all set to walk to Canady and
straight on through New York City if that's how the
chips fall."

"New York City?" Slim yelled. "Did I hear you say?
Ain't this the road west to Pittsburgh?"

Slim stopped, but the man hurried right along. "Say,
did you hear me?" Slim yelled. That old man heard him
all right but didn't care. "Keep walking," I say, "maybe
I'll be in Canady, maybe I won't. Can't wait around all
night." And he kept talkin, and walkin, till all we could
see was his shadow fadin in the dark and gone like a ghost.

"Well," Slim said, "it *was* a ghost." And he worried
himself to death standin there with me in those fearful
river woods, at midnight, tryin to figure where we was
and how we got lost. All I could hear now was the pat
of rain on a million leaves, and the chug-chug across the
river, and my own heart beatin in all that open air. Lord.
It's somethin.

"Why'd I go follow that crazy man!" Slim said, and seemed lonesome, and looked for me, and reached some. "Pic, you there?"

"Slim, I'm scairt," I said.

"Well don't be scairt, we'll walk back to town and get back to those lights and folks can see us. Whoo!"

"Slim, who was that man?" I asked him, and he said, "Shoo, that was some kinda ghost of the river, he's been lookin for Canady in Virginia, West Virginia, West Pennsylvania, North New York, New York City, East Arthuritis and South Pottzawattomy for the last eighty years as far as I can figure, and on foot, too. He'll never find the Canady and he'll never get to Canady because he's goin the wrong way all the time."

So grandpa the next three cars swished by, and the fourth one stopped for us, and we ran for it. Was big solemn white man in a beach-wagon truck. "Yes," he said, "this is the road west to Pittsburgh but you better go back to town for a ride."

"That old man is goin to walk west all night, and he wants to get to the North to Canady," said Slim, and it was the God-awfullest truth, and we was talkin about that Ghost of the Susquehanna for the next three months I tell you when we got to Sheila in San Francisco.

14. HOW WE FINALLY GOT TO CALIFORNY

I'M GOIN TELL YOU IT WAS A LONG TRIP, grandpa. That man rode us back to Harrisburg in the rain. He told us how to take a left and then a right and then left and then right and go down to a lunch wagon where he said they made very good sweet yams and pigs' feet and also seven-inch-long hot dogs with Picadilly Circus on it. Me and Slim went in there and sat down in the eatin part of the restrant, th'other side was a spittoon place with a big bunch of men argufyin about how they was Jindians.

"Don't tell me that, you're no Indian!"

"Oh I ain't, ain't I?—I'm a Pottzawattomy from Canady and my mother was pure-bred Cherokee."

"If you're a Pottzawattomy from Canady and your mother was pure-bredded Cherokee I'm James Roosevelt Turner."

"Well turn around, son, and I'll give you the biggest whompin you ever got." And then there was the sound of glasses breakin, and fights, and hollerin, and women yowlin, and this woman came over to the table where me and Slim was eatin and sat down with us with a nice smile and said "May I join you?" just as a big flock of police-men came in out of a squad car. The woman, girl actelly, said to Slim:

"May I sit?"

And she smiled but Slim he was afeared of the police-men and never smiled back at her smile, besides Slim is married to Sheila, but the woman sat there actin as though she was at the same table with us and no one of the police-men offered up to bother her. Slim didn't say no, and he didn't say yes. The police-men took away the skeedaddlin Jindians and ever'thing was peaceful again.

Me and Slim ate up all our money on candy yams and pigs' knucklets feets and seven-inch-long hot dogs and Slim didn't pay no intention which-however to the woman. It was a barnyard. But you know, grandpa, a whole lot of black men have Jindian blood, as I discovered up when I saw all those Jindians in Nebraskar, Ioway and Nevady, not to mention Oakland.

But now we were pretty well filled up with food-supper and ready to roam on in the rainin, only now it was slower now, pizzlin, and Slim said:

"Now next step is to get to Pittsburgh down this Route 22."

It was early mornin sunrisin and an au-to went by and squished a blue-color bird under the rollin wheel.

It made me sickish to hear the squeak of it. I wished there was a better place. I felt missilated. A plumber gave us a ride to Huntingdon, then a light-bulb man gave us a ride to Holidaysburg, then a man called Biddy Blair gave us a ride to Blairsville, then we wound up in Corapolis with a countryfolk truck driver whose son had jess had a hernia belly. It was awful all them stories you heard. But I had a feelin in my chest that ever'body was doin their best, I guess.

Now it was about seben o'clock in the mornin and Slim bought some Sin-Sins to put sugar in our mouth. He was rare worried he'd never get to Sheila. He didn't not ever tell me how long it was to Oakland for fear I'd get scairt. I told him I didn't know there was so many white people in the world, comin as I done from North Carolina countryfolks.

He said: "Yep."

Then he said: "I wonder if Mr. Otis sent out the cops after me for kidnapin you. Well, he won't find us now. Here's stoppin a car with two men in it."

They was goin eighty miles a hour or somethin like that but they stopped, squeak. We got in the back. They said:

"Where you goin?—Shoot, we Montana-bound, you got money?"

Slim said "Not much so."

So they said "We'll drop you off at Pittsburgh." It was rainin, grandpa, when we got to Pittsburgh. Me and Slim went inta the railroad station, to get out of the rainin. Two men in blue choo-choo master suits told us to get out. So we pulled up our collars and draddled on down the street, we saw a church, with a cross on top on it. Slim said:

"Let's go in there and dry up some. Don't reckon they'll throw us out of there."

It was chilly-like but there was a runnin heat comin from the furnace in the bottom down-belows, and a man upstairs was playin the big organ piano, Slim said it was the Have-a-Maria, and then a fellow come by with a lighted stick and went rush-up lightin candles at the front part, "The Halter," said Slim (said it laughin), and outside it was rainin cats and dogs.

Grandpa, when I heared that music I shushed Slim, and I said:

"Can I sing?"

"Slim wants to know if you know the tune?" said Slim.

"Well I'll jess hum."

Slim said: "Here comes the big man in the black coat."

By this time I was already hummin.

The big man in the black coat said "You have a beautiful voice, what's your name?"

"Pictorial Review Jackson of North Carolina."

"And who's he?"

"My brother John Jackson."

The priest axed "Do you know how to dust pews?"

Slim says "I just worked in a cookie factory and I'd rather dust pews."

"Do you know how to mop floors in the basement? Two Army cots beside the furnace, hundred dollars a month, fifty each, free food, no rent."

Slim says "Tsa deal, we are goin all the way to Californy to join up with my wife."

"What's your wife's name?"

"Sheila Jackson, born Joyner, North Carolina."

"I am Father John McGillicuddy."

Slim sez "Ain't you the guy that managed the Philadelphia Phillies?"

"No, that was Cornelius McGillicuddy, some distant cousin . . . Philadelphia Athletics . . . I am Father John McGillicuddy, Society of Jesus, Jesuit Order. Now little Jackson Picture you want to go up sing in the choir? What's your favorite tune?"

Grandpa I told him *Our Father Which Art in Heaven*, coulda made Lulu cry to hear me sing like that in her porch.

So Father McGillicuddy took me up to the attic LOFT, and sat me by the man with his hands on the keys of the ORGAN. Grandpa, I even whistled and I wished I had my harmonica, and the priest man sang up and said I sung up like an angel.

By the by, Slim was present down at the cellar moppin up the floor, he said he sure wisht he had his horn, but said he found a horn in his little brother's voice.

So we told Father McGillicuddy soon's we pick up one hunnerd dollars pay we would fetch for Oakland on the Greyhound Bus, but Father McGillicuddy said it was comin up close to Sunday mornin, as it was Adventist or adventurous night now, and Saturday too, and wanted me to sing before the intire congregation the Lord's Prayer, which I done, up in the LOFT, like best I could. Father McGillicuddy was s'tickled he was sunrise all over. Them Irish mans is so tickled they's pink as a shoat all over, but I feasable say they got troubles of their own, so we had our hunnerd dollars and took the road bus with the picture of the blue hound dog on the side of it, Greyhound it's called, and we peewetted across Ohia and clear inta Nebraskar, Slim was asleep in the back seat all alone stretched out legs all over, and I was sittin in a reg'lar seat near-up with a ninety-year-old white man, and when we come to a stop just before Kearney, Nebraskar, the old man said to me:

"I gotta go to the toilet."

So I led him out of the bus holdin his hand, 'case he was about to fall in the snow, and ask the gas man where was the men's room. Finished, I took the old man back in the bus, and the bus driver yelled out:

"Somebody's drinkin around here!"

And the bus driver was wearin black gloves. Two men was in the front seat next to him holdin hands together.

Slim was still snorin on the back-seat bed. Then he got up said to me:

"Hi, baby."

First thing you know, no more snow. Heard another old man behind me say "I'm goin back to Oroville and bank my dust."

We then was now in the Sacramenty Valley, grandpa, and quick we saw Sheila's ropelines with wash on hooks of wood hung dryin, flappety-flap.

Slim, he put his two hands on his back, limpied around the yard, and said, "I got Arthur-itis, Bus-itis, Road-itis, Pic-itis and ever' other It-is in the world."

And Sheila run up, kissed him hungarianly, and we went in eat the steak she saved up for us, with mashy potatoes, pole beans, and cherry banana spoon ice cream split.